A Time to Cherish

A Time to Cherish

ROBIN JONES GUNN

BETHANY HOUSE PUBLISHERS
MINNEAPOLIS, MINNESOTA 55438

02 03 04 05 06 07 08 09 / 17 16 15 14 13 12 11 10 9 8 7 6 5

Contents

CHAPTER ONE

No Guarantees

Christy Miller suddenly woke up. She kicked the heavy sleeping bag off her sweaty legs and squinted her eyes in the darkness, trying to remember where she was. Her bed seemed to tilt back and forth with a gentle roll.

Then Christy remembered. She was on a houseboat: Aunt Marti's idea of a Farewell to Summer party over the Labor Day weekend.

She could hear her best friend, Katie, gently snoring across the cabin. Christy pulled on her sweats and placed her bare feet on the cool floor. Padding her way to the boat's front deck, she closed the sliding glass door behind her and drew in a deep breath of fresh morning air.

The sky had not quite awakened but seemed to be slowly rising, rubbing the thin, pink-cloud "sleepers" from its eyes and checking its reflection in the still lake-mirror.

The day promised to be perfect. She could smell it in the sweet breeze rising off the water. Just then something splashed in the water. She quickly figured out it must be either Todd or Doug. The two of them had slept under the stars on the houseboat's roof.

Soon Todd's white-blond head popped up out of the water. He didn't notice Christy watching him and kept swimming with quiet, easy strokes. Turning to float on his back, he spoke into the dawn.

"O Lord, our Lord, how majestic is Your name in all the earth! You have set Your glory above the heavens!"

Christy couldn't help but smile. That was so like Todd.

She moved closer to the railing, wondering if she should interrupt Todd's conversation with God. On her last step, her foot tagged the corner of a folded-up beach chair, causing it to tip over and clatter loudly. Todd spun around in the water and began to swim back toward the houseboat.

Christy quickly smoothed back her nutmeg brown hair and tried to tuck the wild ends into her loose braid. *I probably look awful! Groggy, to say the least.*

Then she realized this was Todd, and he had never been the kind of guy to judge anyone by outward appearances. Hopefully he would keep that in mind when he saw her fresh from her sleeping bag.

Todd grabbed onto one of the ropes hanging from the front of the houseboat and pulled himself up the steps onto the deck.

"Hi," Christy whispered shyly. "How's the water?"

Todd smiled and reached for a beach towel on the railing. His silver-blue eyes met Christy's, and he whispered back, "You want to find out?"

"Not really."

"Not even a little cold shower?" Todd asked, shaking his hair in front of her like a dog.

"Okay, okay," Christy said with a giggle, holding up her hands in defense. "You convinced me; it's cold!"

"Refreshing," Todd corrected her, slipping a navy blue

hooded sweatshirt over his head and sticking his hands in the front pocket. "You the only one up?"

Christy nodded. "I think so."

"It was a long ride here yesterday," Todd reasoned. "They'll probably all sleep in. What got you up this early?"

"I was burning up in my sleeping bag. It must be designed for subzero temperatures."

"I know the perfect way to cool you off. Let's go for a spin around the lake."

"In what?" Christy asked. "If we start up the ski boat, we'll wake everyone."

"Then we'll take the raft," Todd said, pulling the big, yellow inflated monster from the side of the houseboat. He dropped it into the water. "Ladies first."

Christy went through all her mental resistance in record time. Would they get in trouble for going out like this without telling anyone? No, Bob and Marti trusted Todd. What if she got her sweats wet? So what? She could change into something dry when they came back. Unable to think of a reason why she shouldn't go, Christy lowered herself into the wobbly raft.

Todd grabbed two paddles, put up the hood on his sweatshirt, and with the beach towel wrapped around his wet swim trunks, joined Christy. They silently paddled away from the cove and headed for the open part of the lake.

One look at Todd's face and Christy knew he thought this was an adventure. Todd thrived on adventure. His lifelong ambition was to become a missionary and live in the jungle.

Christy liked adventure, too. At least the little bit she had experienced in her seventeen years. But she wasn't sure how she felt about spending the rest of her life in the jungle. Maybe if she had one of those butane curling irons that didn't need to be plugged in.

"Isn't it beautiful?" Todd asked, looking up at the awakening sky. He pointed to a trail of puffy white clouds stomping across the seamless blue. "The clouds are the dust beneath His feet."

Christy smiled at Todd's poetic flair. He looked like a monk with the hood covering his head. "Did you just make that up?" Christy asked.

"No," Todd confessed. "An Old Testament prophet did. Nahum, to be exact. I always think of that verse when I see clouds that look as though God just went for a morning stroll across the face of the earth."

Christy knew the look in Todd's eyes. She had seen it many times during the two years she had known him. Two years filled with more ups and downs than an elevator. Yet one thing had never changed: Todd's love for God. More than once Christy had wished Todd would become even one-tenth as committed to her as he was to God.

It wasn't that she didn't love God, too. She did. She had promised her heart to the Lord more than two years ago and had grown a lot as a Christian since then. But all Todd had ever promised her was that they would be friends forever. What did that mean?

Next week she would begin her senior year in high school, and Todd was now a sophomore in college. How old did a guy have to be before he made a substantial promise to a girl?

"You know what this reminds me of?" Todd asked. "That morning on the beach."

"You mean Christmas morning a couple of years ago when we made breakfast and the sea gulls scarfed it all?" Christy said.

Todd smiled. "I almost forgot about that. No, I mean that

morning last year. Remember? We just happened to meet on the beach in the fog.''

A knot tightened in Christy's stomach. That was not a morning she liked to remember. "And here we are,'' she said, ignoring the knot, "out together again at the break of day. Only this time you're not telling me you're going off to Hawaii indefinitely to surf.'' Christy hesitated. "Or are you?''

"Nope,'' Todd said, putting down his paddle and letting the raft float. He propped his hands behind his head and leaned back against the pudgy side of the raft. "And you're not trying to give me back your ID bracelet, either.''

Christy glanced down at the gold bracelet on her right wrist. The engraved word "Forever'' glinted in the rising sun. "I wanted you to be free to go to Hawaii and not feel obligated to me.''

"And I wanted you to be free to date Rick and not feel like I was holding you back,'' Todd countered.

Christy sighed. "I wish now that you had held me back. I don't have pleasant memories of dating Rick.''

"Had to be your own choice,'' Todd said. "No one else could make that decision for you. That would be robbing you of who you are. There's great value in everything that happened. You just have to look for it.''

Christy leaned back and felt the sun warming the left side of her face. She thought hard about Rick and his overpowering ways, wondering what possible great value had come out of their relationship. Maybe going with Rick had taught her more about the kind of guy she *did* want to be with. Now, more than ever, Todd was definitely that guy.

"What would you like from me, Christy?'' Todd suddenly asked, as if he had been reading her thoughts.

"What do you mean?''

"You want more of a commitment than what we have now, don't you?"

Christy felt her cheeks turn red—and not because of the sun. "Why do you say that?"

"Your aunt had a little talk with me on the way up yesterday when you were in the truck with Katie and Doug. She told me that if I didn't stake my claim soon, you'd take off with some other guy. She thinks it's time we officially start going together, let people know we're a couple."

Now Christy felt really embarrassed. Aunt Marti was always speaking her mind, but Todd never seemed to pay much attention to her. Why was he bringing all this up now?

"Todd, you know my aunt. That's her idea, not mine."

"Yeah, I know, that's what she said."

Christy shook her head. "Todd, I apologize—"

"No need. I would have let it go except Doug has been asking me about our relationship. I guess you know he's been wanting to go out with you for a long time."

"Doug?"

Todd nodded. "You mean you didn't know?"

"No. I was hoping he and Katie would get together."

Todd shrugged. For several long minutes it was quiet.

"So," Todd said, leaning forward and looking Christy in the eye, "I guess I'm feeling like we have to start making some decisions about us. What do you really think, Kilikina? Do you want more of a commitment from me?"

Christy always melted inside when Todd called her by her Hawaiian name. For a long time she had wished he would ask her this kind of question. But she hadn't expected it. Not here. Not this morning. If it weren't for her bare feet being nearly numb from the puddle of cool water in the raft, she would have thought she was still asleep, and all this was a romantic dream.

"I don't know," she said, surprised to hear such a wishy-washy answer pop out.

"Then tell me how you feel."

"About you?"

"About me, about us. I need to know what you're thinking and feeling."

"Well, I feel really good when I'm with you," Christy began. "Really comfortable. I miss you when I don't see you. I think about you all the time, and I pray for you every day. You make me feel closer to God, and I never feel pressured to try to be anything other than myself around you. I like you more than any other guy I've ever known."

A slow smile crept onto Todd's face. It was as if Christy's words were warming him from the inside out. She had never been able to tell him so clearly how she felt about him. It felt good to put her heart out there in the open. She had tried doing the same thing a year ago at their early morning encounter on the beach, but it obviously wasn't the right time. Todd wouldn't receive her words last year. This morning they made him glow.

"I feel the same way about you," Todd said. "It's been important to me all along that we take things slowly. I never wanted our relationship to grow too fast."

"Two years is not exactly too fast," Christy said with a teasing smile.

"Just about right, I'd say. That's the way it is with God, you know. He's always on time but rarely early."

Christy couldn't believe how smoothly this conversation was going. She and Todd didn't talk about their feelings very often. A hint of apprehension and excitement started to hedge in.

It was silent again as the morning ripples on the lake gently rocked their raft back and forth. Todd broke the quiet with a nervous chuckle. "I don't know how to say it. What's the term for us? Are we now officially 'going together' or what?"

"I don't know, are we?" Christy asked cautiously.

"That's what you want, isn't it?"

"Yes, I mean, if that's what you want."

"That's what I want," Todd said firmly. "I want to be your boyfriend, even though I hate using that term. You reflect what's in the heart. Something doesn't come from inside you simply because you speak it into being. If it's truly in your heart, it will come out in what you do."

Christy nodded. She knew exactly what Todd meant. Their relationship had always been beyond labels. Todd had consistently been true to his word to be her friend, no matter what happened.

"So now we're officially a couple," Todd said, squaring his broad shoulders and smiling so the dimple showed on his right cheek. "Do you feel any different?"

"No, not exactly."

"Neither do I. Maybe that's good. Maybe everything is still at the same level with us, only now we have an answer to give everyone else. We're going together."

Christy liked the sound of Todd's deep voice saying, "We're going together." She loved the feeling of being more secure in their relationship.

"I'm glad," she told him softly.

"Me too," Todd said, then tenderly added, "You are an incredible person, Kilikina. I hold you in my heart. You are the only girl I've ever kissed. I haven't been the same since that night right after we met and I followed you out to the jetty when you left Shawn's party."

"I felt like such a baby that night," Christy remembered. "Everyone was drinking, and I was so naive!"

"You were innocent, Christy. You have no idea how beautiful that made you."

Christy felt like crying. "Todd, I . . ." She didn't know how to put into words everything she felt right then. "I'm really glad, I mean, this is so . . . I don't know. It's so *right*. I'm really happy we're moving our relationship forward."

Just then the roar from a ski boat engine broke their magical moment. Todd squinted and then started to wave at the boat. "It's Doug and Katie. I bet he's ready to start some serious water skiing!"

Doug cut the engine on the boat and slowly drifted toward the raft. "Ahoy, mates!" he called out. Doug wore a bandana "pirate style" around his short, sandy blond hair. The broad smile that spread across his face showed he was in his typically great mood. "Would ye be needin' a hoist back to the cove before ye find yourselves shipwrecked?"

Todd turned to Christy and said, "That wouldn't be so bad, would it?"

"Which?" Christy asked. "Being hoisted back to shore or being shipwrecked?"

Todd didn't answer, and for a moment the two of them locked gazes, their eyes revealing a thousand secrets of the heart.

"I think we're interrupting something," Katie said, her red hair swishing as she looked at Christy and Todd and then at Doug. She held up an orange flag used to indicate a downed skier in the water. Waving it like a fairy wand, she asked, "Tell us, you two, what did we miss out on this morning? Anything you'd like to share with the rest of us?"

Christy felt herself blushing again and wondered how old she would be before she outgrew this reflex.

"We've been checking out the dust of God's feet," Todd answered. "And making some promises," he added in a whisper loud enough for only Christy to hear.

"So how about us making some of our own wave-dust?" Doug asked. "You ready to break up some of this glass?"

"Wait! We want you to tow us first," Katie yelled. "Let me get in the raft with Christy, and you guys can tow us back to the houseboat."

"As long as you promise to go *slow!*" Christy said.

Doug threw out a long rope for Todd to secure the raft to the back of the boat while Katie made the transfer from boat to raft. Todd climbed up the stepladder by the rudder and tightened the knot on the rope.

"Okay, here are the signals," Todd said. "Thumbs up means go faster. A finger across your throat like this means stop, and a thumb down means slow down."

Christy put her thumb down. "I mean it, you guys, go slow!"

"You'd better find something to hold on to," Todd called from the boat. He tossed two orange life vests into the raft and instructed them to put them on.

Christy fastened the vest over her sweats and grabbed onto a black handle on the side of the raft. "Whose idea was this anyway?"

"Mine," Katie said without regret. Then looking into Christy's blue-green eyes, Katie said, "What?"

"What, what?" Christy repeated back to her.

"What's up with you?"

"What do you mean?"

Katie put her hand on her hip, tilted her head, and examined her best friend's expression. "I was right. There was something going on between you two this morning. You have a secret, Christina Juliet Miller, don't you?"

Christy didn't answer with words, but the smile skipping across her lips gave it all away.

"I knew it!" Katie cried loud enough to awaken any lazy fish who weren't up yet. "Don't tell me; let me guess. You and Todd are finally going together! Am I right?"

Christy looked up into the boat, hoping to see Todd's assuring grin. Instead, she saw Doug's usually smiling face transformed into a grim frown.

Just then Doug started up the boat with a roar. The rope pulled tight, and the raft lurched in the water.

Christy let out a scream and yelled, "Go slow!"

Doug jammed the ski boat into high. Their raft felt as if it suddenly became airborne. The girls held on, screaming and trying to motion the "slow down" and "stop" signals to the guys.

Doug turned to the right, and the raft flew over a wave and skittered outside the wake. Before they could get their balance, another, larger wave rushed up from underneath the raft, flipping the girls into the water.

Their life vests brought them bobbing up to the surface at the same time, and Katie and Christy began to tread water and hurl threats at the guys.

"Doug did that on purpose!" Katie said as the boat slowly motored in a circle to come back and retrieve them. "And I have several ideas of how we can get him back this weekend."

Even across the sparkling water, Christy could recognize the mischievous glint in the eyes of her red-haired friend.

"I leave all the revenge games to you," Christy said, aware of how heavy her soaked sweats had become as she kicked her legs in the water. "I don't want to start anything unless there's a guarantee I won't get hurt in the end."

Katie tilted back her head and laughed. "It's too late for that!"

Christy was now next to Katie in the water. The guys threw them a rope.

"One dunk in the lake by Doug doesn't mean it's too late," Christy said.

"Oh, I didn't mean Doug," Katie answered. "I meant with Todd. Something happened with you two this morning. I can tell. And whatever it was, I have a feeling it's too late for any kind of a guarantee you won't get hurt in the end."

CHAPTER TWO

Just Enjoy Today

When the foursome arrived back at the houseboat, Uncle Bob called to them from the window above the kitchen sink, "You're just in time for pancakes. Could you smell them out there on the lake?"

The guys docked the boat, and the soaked girls wrung out the bottoms of their shirts one more time before stepping onto the deck.

"The guys want to go back out skiing while it's still calm," Katie told Bob.

"No problem. Breakfast is served all morning long in my galley." He opened the sliding screen door and, taking a good look at Christy, asked, "Are you planning to enter some kind of contest for drowned rats that I didn't know about?"

"The only drowned rat contest around here," Katie informed him, "is going to involve two certain young pirates."

"Anybody we know?" Bob asked, his merry eyes twinkling. For a man in his fifties who had never had children of his own, Bob always seemed to enjoy Christy and her friends. His easygoing manner made him everyone's favorite adopted uncle. The only one who ever had run-ins with Bob was Aunt Marti, but then, she had tiffs with everyone at one point or another.

"Come on, Katie!" Doug called out from the boat. "We need you to come with us to hold the flag."

"My public beckons me," Katie said, dramatically placing the back of her hand against her forehead. "Oh, the price of popularity!"

Christy giggled at her fun-loving friend. "Go answer your call, Katie. I shall stay behind to put on dry clothes and stuff my face with pancakes. Do you want a dry T-shirt?"

"Not a bad idea. Throw me a towel, too."

As soon as the boat left with Katie vigorously waving the flag in a playful farewell, Christy changed into her bathing suit and a big T-shirt. Undoing her matted braid, she joined Bob in the kitchen and began to brush out her soaked hair. The excess water dripped onto the floor as she flipped her hair down so she could brush it from the underside.

"Gorgeous day," Bob said, scooping another round of sourdough blueberry pancakes onto the already heaping platter. "Couldn't have asked for better weather."

"Good morning, all!" Aunt Marti called out, opening the door to their back bedroom.

Just then Christy flipped her long hair over to hang down her back. Beads of water, launched from the ends of her hair, flew across the small kitchen and, as if they had been directed at Marti, all hit the target.

"Oh, stop that this instant!" Marti said with a squeal.

Christy turned to see her petite aunt adorned in a perky little sailor shirt with sprinkles of water all over it. Even her perfectly styled short, dark hair now had moisture clinging to the bangs. "I'm so sorry, Aunt Marti. I didn't mean to do that."

"It's all right," Bob said, jumping in with a towel for his indignant wife. "Just a little morning wake-up for you, Martha. I hear it works better than a cup of coffee."

"I was already awake, thank you," Marti replied stiffly, snatching the towel from Bob's hands. Scanning the room, she asked, "Where are the boys?"

"Out skiing with Katie," Bob said.

Marti's expression changed. It seemed she wasn't quite as upset once she realized her only audience had been Bob and Christy.

Giving her flawless makeup one more pat with the towel, Marti turned to Christy with a scowl and said, "You might consider doing your hair in the bathroom for the remainder of the trip."

"I will. And I'm sorry. I didn't see you."

Bob handed Marti a mug of coffee and said, "Vanilla hazelnut, your favorite. Are you ready for some breakfast?"

Marti accepted the peace offering and sat down at the table. Christy sat across from her and helped herself to three steaming pancakes.

"These sure smell good," she said, hoping Marti's sour mood would pass quickly, especially before Christy's friends returned. She had seen many of Marti's moods come and go over the years, and she knew a lot of it was just her aunt's personality. Still, Christy couldn't help but feel grinding guilt in the pit of her stomach, as if she were responsible for whether or not Marti was in a good mood.

"It was a beautiful sunrise this morning," Christy said, hoping to get the conversation moving. "Are you going to eat with us, Uncle Bob?"

He looked at the three pancakes browning in the skillet and, turning off the burner, said, "Sure. I suppose we have enough to get us started here." Bob plopped the hotcakes onto his plate and slid into a chair at the head of the table.

"Would you guys mind if we prayed?" Christy asked. She had been through this a number of times, since her aunt and uncle weren't the pray-before-meals kind of people. Christy had decided she wouldn't give up praying around them just because they didn't normally do it.

Bob and Marti exchanged glances before respectfully bowing their heads. Christy prayed aloud, thanking God for their safe trip, for the beautiful day, for the food and then for Katie, the guys, Bob, and Marti. When she looked up after saying "Amen," Marti already had her head up and was glaring at her.

"A person's food could go cold waiting for you to pray your blessings on the world," Marti said.

Obviously she hadn't snapped out of her bad mood yet. Christy decided it would be best not to say anything for a while and set to work cutting her pancakes.

"How you can eat like that and stay slim is beyond my understanding," Marti said, sipping her coffee, which apparently would be her entire breakfast. "I hope you're working on your thighs like I told you. It has always been a problem for the women in our family, and you can see how your mother's thighs have succumbed to heredity. Make sure you don't sit back and let the same thing happen to you."

Christy put a large bite of pancake in her mouth and enjoyed it thoroughly before saying, "Actually, Aunt Marti, I think my mother is just fine the way she is, and I think I'm fine just the way I am. As long as a person is healthy, I don't think it should matter what their body shape is."

"You may not care, but men certainly care. Keep that in mind if you think you're going to attract a young man simply because you're 'healthy.' "

"I don't have to worry about attracting young men," Christy said under her breath. She knew better than to drop hints to her aunt. Especially hints about Todd. Especially if she wanted it to remain a secret. Still, the news that she and Todd were now going together would probably snap Marti out of her critical mood.

"What did you say, Christina? I couldn't hear you."

Christy put down her fork and took a deep breath. "I guess you both would be interested to know that Todd and I had a talk about our relationship this morning, and—"

Marti clasped her hands together and said, "I knew it! I knew he'd take my . . . I mean that Todd would take the initiative to cement your relationship. This is wonderful, Christy!"

"Well, nothing is really different except maybe that we've defined things."

"So now you two are promised to each other. This is wonderful!" Marti's whole countenance had changed from gloom to sunshine.

"We're not 'promised,' " Christy corrected her. "We're 'going together.' That's how Todd phrased it."

"This is absolutely perfect," Marti said triumphantly. "You're going steady! That is the first step, and for you two, it's definitely the next step." She pushed away her coffee cup and leaned across the table to give Christy her insights. "A steady boyfriend your senior year will make things so much easier for you. Football games, Christmas banquets, the prom—you'll never have to worry about having a date. When you graduate, Todd will have two more years of college, and you two should attend the same university during that time. I prefer something close to home. Perhaps Irvine or UCLA. You can get married the summer after your sophomore year since Todd will be graduated. Then, while you finish your last two years, Todd can complete his master's. It's just perfect!"

Christy couldn't help but laugh. "You have it all figured out, don't you? But what if that's not what God wants?"

Marti looked surprised. "Why wouldn't it be? Doesn't God want the best for you? I think even God would have to agree that Todd is the best for you."

Christy laughed again at her aunt's theology. "I think God gives His best to those who leave the choice up to Him."

Marti processed that thought for a minute and was about to counter with a comment when Bob spoke up. "Just enjoy today, Christy. None of us knows what the future holds. You need to live for today and let everything come as it will."

"There's certainly nothing wrong in planning for the future," Marti said. "If Christy doesn't think through these important steps now, she might make some terrible mistakes she'll regret the rest of her life."

"But she doesn't need to make all of those choices today," Bob said softly. Turning back toward Christy, he reached for her hand, gave it a squeeze, and said, "We're real happy for you, Bright Eyes. Todd's a lucky guy to have a young lady like you in his life. I'll make sure he realizes how lucky he is."

"And you make sure you're always worthy of him," Marti advised. "There aren't many like him left in this world."

"I know," Christy said, feeling her heart warming at the thought of Todd.

But in the back corner of Christy's mind, Katie's words of warning hung like a small, gray storm cloud heading her direction. Christy brushed the thought away. What did Katie know about relationships, anyway? She had never even had a boyfriend. Maybe all that would change this weekend, if Doug would only notice what a treasure Katie was.

"More pancakes?" Bob offered.

"Not for me," Christy said. "They were sure good. I imagine the guys will put away what's left."

Christy's prediction was correct. Todd ate at least fourteen pancakes, and she lost count with Doug somewhere after twenty-three. Katie kept up until the guys hit the double digits.

"These are the best pancakes I've ever had," Katie said, wiping her mouth. "They must be loaded with sugar for me to like them so much. Sugar is one of my four basic food groups, you know."

"You kids think you're ready for some more water fun?" Bob asked. "I'm ready to take the boat out for a bit. Anyone want to go with me?"

All four of them eagerly took Bob up on the offer. When Christy climbed into the boat, she sat in the first available seat, which happened to be next to Doug. As soon as she sat down, Doug popped up. Without looking at Christy, he said, "I imagine you'd rather sit by Todd. I'll move."

What's wrong with him? He wouldn't look at me during breakfast, either. He's acting pretty immature for a college student. Just because Katie announced Todd and I are going together, doesn't mean Doug and I can't still be close friends.

Todd was the last one to board, and he took the empty seat next to Christy. "You want to get some skiing in first, Bob? Doug or I would be glad to drive if you do."

"You guys go ahead. I'd like to get a feel for the lake first. Who's up? Doug?"

"Sure, I'll go. I'm ready to try one ski this time," Doug said. He buckled up his life vest, and when Bob stopped the boat in the deeper water, Doug jumped into the lake. It took him only a few minutes to secure both feet in the one ski and get into position. "Okay, hit it!" he yelled, and Bob obliged by charging the boat through the blue water. Doug got right up and balanced on the ski as if he had done it a hundred times before.

"Are you sure he's never gone on one ski before?" Katie asked. "Look at him; he looks like a pro!"

Doug appeared to become braver as he slid from side to side behind the boat, each time bouncing over the curling wake. Bob zipped around the lake more aggressively when he saw how well Doug handled each twist and turn.

One sharp turn to the right brought them head-on with the wake of a speed boat that had just passed. The impact of the water caused their boat to rise up and come down hard. For Doug, the crashing waves created behind the boat proved disastrous, and he took a big tumble.

"We should have had that one on camera," Katie exclaimed, lifting the flag high as Bob slowed way down and circled back to pick up Doug. "Wasn't he fantastic?" Then louder, so Doug could hear from his crouched position in the water, "You were fantastic, Doug! Wish I had a picture."

He waved to Katie, and it seemed to Christy that his cheerful disposition was returning. Once he climbed back in the boat, his laughter convinced Christy that whatever was bothering him had somehow been left behind during his successful skim across the lake. Shivering, smiling, and soaking wet, Doug bent over Katie and gave her one of his famous hugs before looking for his towel.

"There," he said, "now you're ready to get the rest of yourself wet and show us how *you* do on one ski."

"You eel!" Katie cried, shaking her arms to remove the wet. "I'll show you! I'll make your run look like a cartoon clip. Stand back, everyone. I'm a woman on a mission." Katie handed the flag to Christy, buckled up her life vest, and jumped into the water. "Throw me that ski, Mr. Big Shot. You're about to be humbled."

Clearly unafraid of anything requiring athletic ability, Katie tried three times to get up. Each time she lost her balance and surfaced to the roar of Doug's heckling. The fourth attempt proved to be the winner, and as soon as she gained her balance, Katie leaned back and confidently let go with one hand to wave to the crew.

"She's going to eat it big time," Doug said, his eyes glued on Katie's overly confident frame as she jumped over the wake and came down hard on the ski. She retained her balance. "I don't believe it! She's a maniac!"

Christy couldn't help but admire Katie. She was really good. Anything she ever attempted in the realm of sports came to her easily. It was the opposite for Christy. The worst part was knowing that some time during this weekend she would have to try water skiing. None of these guys would accept "I don't feel like it."

Her chance came all too soon. Katie showed off for a good ten minutes before she tried one daring stunt too many and crashed into the water. "You're next, Christy" were Katie's first words as she climbed back into the boat. "The water is warm. Really."

"I'll go in with her," Todd volunteered. "It's easier to figure out the right position the first time when you have someone in the water with you."

Now Christy knew she couldn't put off the inevitable. Not when Todd was willing to do all he could to help her. She fastened her life vest and, reaching for Todd's assuring hand, jumped into the water by his side.

"Brrr!" she called out as soon as she surfaced. "What do you mean the water is warm, Katie? It's freezing!"

"No it isn't," Katie called back. "You'll get used to it. Believe me, once your adrenaline kicks in, you won't feel a thing."

"Here you go," Todd said, holding the two skis in place above the water. "Put your arm around my shoulder and start with the right foot."

It was a clumsy sensation for Christy, trying to balance while buoyant and maneuvering a long water ski onto each foot. Todd patiently helped her get both skis on and instructed her to "sit" in the water with the tow rope wedged between the skis. "Keep both skis pointed up," he said. "Try to sort of sit on the back of them, and when the boat pulls you out of the water, lean back. Your natural reflex will be to let go when you feel the tug, but just hang on, point your toes toward the boat, and lean back."

Christy shivered and let out a bewildered sigh. "That's a lot to remember."

"You can do it. Relax. This is fun."

"It is?"

Todd laughed and started to swim back to the boat. Christy waited in the water, feeling uncomfortable with the life vest pushing up to her ears and her ankles bent at a weird angle in the skis.

Todd climbed in the boat and waved to her. "Are you ready?"

"I guess," Christy called out.

"Say 'hit it' when you're ready," Katie informed her.

She didn't feel ready. Still, she truly wanted to do this. She would love to frolic over the waves like Katie had.

With a quick mental review of all she was supposed to do, Christy yelled, "Hit it, but go slow!"

The "go slow" part was lost in the roar of the motor starting up, and as soon as the taut tow rope lurched forward, Christy let go. Bob turned the boat around, and as they circled, Todd tossed the tow rope to her.

"Remember? You hold on, point your toes, and lean back."

"Right. I've got it this time," Christy said, lacing the rope between her pointed skis. Before she had time to entertain any doubts, she yelled, "Go ahead, hit it!"

This time she held on with all her might and kept her skis pointed straight. Before she knew it, she was up. She was actually standing on both skis, and the skis were gliding across the water. There was only one problem—she was still in a sitting position, bent at the waist, her arms out straight, and her rear end sticking up in the air.

"Stand up!" she could hear her friends calling from the boat. "Lean back!"

The pull of the rope was too strong. She couldn't pull herself to a standing up position, let alone lean back. She continued her ride across the lake with knees bent, arms out straight, and head down, feeling as though she were flying with her legs in cement blocks.

Then, without warning, she lost her balance and dove face first into the unfriendly water. The skis flew off. She let go of the rope, and in an attempt to scream, she swallowed enough lake water to fill a goldfish bowl. Worst of all, half the water had entered through her nose. She felt as though all her eyelashes had been peeled off in the process.

Bob was the only one not laughing when the boat drew near to retrieve her. "You want to try again?" he asked calmly, as if she hadn't just made a major spectacle of herself.

"I don't think so," Christy answered, coughing up big bubbles of lake water and trying not to cry.

"Grab this rope," Todd said. "Pull yourself to the ladder at the back, but be careful the rope doesn't get tangled."

It took a lot of effort to climb into the boat because her arms were quivering and her ankles felt as though they were still locked in cement. Todd had jumped into the water and was calmly fitting the skis on for his turn, as if nothing unusual had happened during Christy's attempt.

It was Katie who offered Christy a helping hand to get her back on board. Katie was still laughing, her green cat eyes brimming with tears of hilarity. "I always knew you were athletically impaired, Christy, but that was the funniest thing I have ever seen!"

Christy felt like telling Katie to just shut up, but she swallowed her anger and reached for a towel to bury her face in. It was bad enough to have gone through such a humiliating experience with people she knew watching her; she didn't need Katie's insults as well.

From the water Todd called out, "Hit it," and Bob cranked up the boat. With the greatest of ease, Todd rose to his feet the first time and made his jaunt around the lake. Baby stuff. Anybody could do it. Anybody but Christy.

Katie *was* right. She was athletically impaired. The only sort of athletic thing she had ever done well was trying out for cheerleader. Christy had worked hard for weeks to get the routines down just right. Maybe she could ski too, if she really tried and gave herself time.

Wrapping the towel around herself, Christy decided whether she learned to ski or not didn't matter. What mattered was that she gave it her best try, knowing it would be harder for her than for her friends.

Christy watched Todd riding smoothly behind the boat. She wondered if everything in her life was going to be harder for her than it was for her friends. She hoped she would always have the courage to at least try.

A slow grin forced its way across her lips as she thought of how she must have looked out there, bent at the waist, skimming across the water like some kind of contestant in a contortionist contest. It reminded her of when she and Katie had taken snow skiing lessons, and Christy had slid out of control and crashed into the ski instructor. The two friends had laughed together over that incident for the rest of the day. She realized she needed to lighten up. To laugh at herself. To take her uncle's advice and just enjoy today.

They spent the rest of the morning on the lake and were ready for lunch when they returned to the houseboat sometime in the early afternoon. Marti scolded them for being gone so long and not checking in.

Todd gave her a side hug and said, "You should have known we were okay. It's only when we never come back that you need to worry."

Marti smiled up at her favorite young man. "Now what kind of sense does that make, Todd? In the future you need to give me a better time reference so I won't have to worry."

Todd reached for a tortilla chip from the open bag Katie offered to him and, crunching loudly, said, "Okay, Marti. Just to make you happy we'll set a time. Or better yet, why don't you come out on the boat with us?"

Marti thought it over while Todd stepped to the table and began to make himself a sandwich from the fixings Bob was setting out.

"I suppose I should go out at least once this weekend."

"After lunch, maybe?" Todd challenged.

"Maybe. As long as it's with just you and Christy." Then with a proud look she added, "My favorite new couple."

Doug, who was sitting at the table spreading mayonnaise on his bread, suddenly stood up, pushed his chair back with his heel, and disappeared out the sliding door. No one seemed to notice except Christy. The rest of them dove into their sandwich making, but Christy's heart was beating hard.

She felt responsible for Doug's reactions. Doug had always been like a big brother to her. She couldn't stand to see him acting like this, and she knew she would be miserable the rest of the weekend if she didn't talk to him.

Gathering her courage, Christy drew away from the group and slipped out onto the deck in search of Doug.

CHAPTER THREE

Marooned!

Christy made her way around the narrow walk on the side of the deck and cautiously approached Doug, who was at the front of the houseboat, shaking out a beach towel.

"Hi," Christy said. "Are you okay?"

"Sure," Doug said, turning to face her. "Why shouldn't I be?"

Christy thought he looked angry. "Are you sure?"

The corners of Doug's mouth turned up into a smile. "Sure as sure can be. I came out for a towel so I wouldn't get the seat wet from my trunks."

"Oh." Christy wasn't sure what else to say. "Good idea."

She thought of their trip up to the lake the day before and how Doug had teased her and given her at least two hugs along the way. Today he hadn't come within ten feet of her. It wasn't her imagination. Something was wrong.

"Doug, somehow I don't believe you. Can't you be honest with me?"

Releasing a sigh, Doug folded his arms across his broad chest and leaned against the railing. "Okay. You want honest? You and Todd getting together has made me feel something."

"What?"

"I don't know. Don't get me wrong, I'm really happy for both of you. I just don't want things to change between us now."

"Nothing is going to change."

"Maybe, maybe not. I've had friends who suddenly became invisible when they started going with a girl. And I have a hard time staying friends with a girl once she's 'taken.'"

"It won't be like that with us," Christy promised. "Todd and I will still both be close friends with you."

"Promise?" Doug asked.

"Yes."

"I confess I'm skeptical, but for now I'll accept that. Let's not talk about this any more and just see how things go. I'm starving! How about you?"

Christy laughed. "How could you be after all those pancakes?"

Doug shrugged and opened the sliding door, motioning for Christy to go first.

After lunch Katie wanted to ski and Christy wanted to lay out on the flat roof of the houseboat. Doug said he was up for more boating, and Todd said he would do "whatever." It seemed like the perfect chance to let Doug and Katie go out on the boat alone. Then Marti stepped in.

"But Todd and Christy haven't taken me out yet in the boat. I suppose I really should go while the weather is nice." Marti reached for her wide-brimmed straw hat. "I only want to go out for a quick motor around the lake."

"Then let's go," Todd said obligingly. "You up for it, Christy?"

"Sure," she said, casting a quick glance at Katie as if to nudge her to spend the time getting closer to Doug. "Let me grab my sunglasses."

Todd helped Marti onto the boat. As soon as her foot touched the deck, a cloud hid the sun. Just as quickly as the cloud blew in, it blew away, and the afternoon sun beat down on Christy's back as she stepped onto the boat.

"I'm going to take the houseboat that direction," Bob told Todd, pointing to the right. "I thought I'd find a new cove for us to park in tonight. It should be easy to locate us when you come back."

Todd nodded and called out, "Later." He started up the engine and slowly headed for the open part of the lake. "You ladies mind putting on life vests? It's boating rules, you know."

"We won't need them," Marti reasoned. "We're only going for a jaunt, and I certainly don't plan on getting wet."

Christy followed Todd's example and slipped on a vest, leaving it unhooked. If nothing else, the vest cut down some of the breeze as they left their protected cover.

For the next fifteen minutes, Marti held on to her hat and directed Todd where to go. He followed her commands and turned into what looked like a long finger of Lake Shasta that was too narrow for houseboats.

Another cloud covered up the sun, and Christy shivered. She wished she had worn more than her damp bathing suit and T-shirt.

Todd steered the boat down the narrowing waterway, pointing out some little hidden coves off to the left.

"Let's go over there," Marti suggested. "Might be a good place for a picnic lunch tomorrow."

Todd expertly pulled the boat into the first hidden cove they came to. Then he jumped into the waist-deep water to secure the boat and called to Marti and Christy to join him in exploring their secret cove.

"How do I get to shore without getting wet?" Marti asked after she watched Christy slide into the water and slosh her way ashore.

"You have to get wet," Todd said. "It's not that deep. Go down the rope ladder on the side."

Christy watched as her aunt hesitated, deliberated, and finally decided to make the sacrifice and join the two of them on the pebbly beach.

"Oh," she screeched when her foot first felt the water, "it's so cold!"

"You're doing great," Todd said, wading out and offering her a hand into shore.

A huge cloud covered the sun. Everything around them seemed unusually quiet and still.

"It feels as if we're a hundred miles from the rest of the world," Christy said, surveying the surroundings. The small beach extended only twenty or so feet behind them before sloping up into a hill. The hillside was sparsely vegetated at its beginning but soon sprouted thick clumps of tall, straight trees that all pointed to the sky like a line of steady, green soldiers. "This is beautiful," Christy said.

"A bit chilly," Marti noticed. "What happened to our sunshine?"

"Let's go exploring," Todd suggested.

"It's too dangerous," Marti said. "We should get going so we can find the houseboat before a storm breaks out. I've heard the weather on a lake can be very unpredictable. Come now. Let's go."

"Shh," Todd whispered. "Did you see that?" He had his back to Marti and was scanning the forest behind them. "Over there, it's a deer! See? Up to the left, behind those two trees."

Christy spotted it and slowly moved closer to Todd. "It's watching us. Isn't it cute? Too bad we don't have some apples to feed it."

"What are you talking about? I don't see anything." Marti marched over toward Todd and Christy, but her sudden movements startled the deer back into the shadows.

"It's gone now," Todd said. "If we come back tomorrow for a picnic, let's be sure to bring some apples."

"Fine," Marti said, sounding irritated. "You can bring it apples tomorrow. Right now, let's get back to the houseboat."

Christy realized how miserable her aunt was, being out of her comfort zone like this. Christy knew the houseboating idea had been Bob's, but he had talked Marti into it by showing her in the brochure that the houseboat contained all the comforts of home. Apparently Marti had experienced enough of the great outdoors by coming to shore and was now ready to go back to her "home" and all those comforts.

The three of them boarded the boat, and Christy had to agree that it felt a little isolated and almost spooky in this silent cove, especially since the sun kept sliding behind the clouds. Todd waited until Christy and Marti were seated and then turned the key in the ignition. Nothing happened. He tried again; a slow, grinding sound emerged. Todd pushed a couple of switches and tried the key again. Nothing.

"What's wrong?" Marti demanded. "What's wrong with the boat?"

Todd tapped his finger on one of the oval gauges and calmly answered, "It appears we're out of gas."

"Out of gas! Didn't you bring an extra can along?"

"No."

"How could you let this happen? After all the skiing you did this morning, didn't you think to check it before we left?"

"No, I didn't."

"We're marooned!" Marti wailed.

Christy felt a little distressed, but nothing close to what her aunt was expressing. As a matter of fact, Marti would have made a great character on the old TV sitcom "Gilligan's Island."

"What are you going to do?" Marti asked. "No one will ever find us in here!"

"I'm going to pray," Todd said matter-of-factly. "Care to join me?"

"I will," Christy offered, getting up from her seat and joining Todd in the front of the boat. The two of them prayed simply and sincerely for God to send help.

Twenty minutes later, Christy pulled the life vest closer around her. It was getting colder, and she wished they had at least brought beach towels along to wrap their legs in.

Todd and Christy were the only ones talking to each other. Marti had covered herself with a life vest and sat huddled on the vinyl seat looking miserable and not saying a word, which Christy had decided was a good thing. Hearing what Marti was thinking right now would not bring much joy to their situation.

Another twenty or thirty minutes passed. The sun continued to play its peek-a-boo game with the clouds, and now no one was saying much of anything. Christy thought how ironic it was that earlier that morning Todd had whispered to her that being shipwrecked wouldn't be such a bad thing. He must not have factored Aunt Marti into the scenario.

Then, as if the volcano inside Marti could hold back no longer, she let forth a steady flow of fiery accusations. Christy had never seen her aunt this mad.

"That's it!" Marti concluded. "You have to go for help, Todd.

I don't care how you do it. Walk over this hill to the other side
or swim out to the main part of the lake. It will be dark soon, and
I refuse to sit here and wait to be eaten by wild animals!''

Christy knew they had at least three hours of sunlight left,
and the only wildlife they had seen was the timid deer. Still, she
knew better than to challenge her aunt's fears. She wondered if
she should go with Todd or stay with her aunt. She knew what
she would rather do.

"We'll wait here," Todd said calmly yet with settled authority,
as if he had already thought through all the options.

Marti looked furious. Not many people opposed her even in
the best of circumstances. "I suppose you're waiting for God to
send an angel to rescue us."

"Angel, human, either one will do."

"This faith thing of yours has gone too far, Todd. It's fine
when you want to have theological discussions with Bob, but
when people's lives are at stake . . ."

Todd put out a hand to silence her. He seemed to be listening
for something. Christy turned her head and listened, too.

"I'm not finished! You *will* listen to what I have to say, Todd
Spencer, if it's the last thing you do before we perish in this stupid
boat."

Todd stood up and, still listening, made his way past Marti to
the back of the boat.

"Will you at least have the courtesy to look at me when I am
talking to you? You can't keep trusting God to do for you what
you should be doing for yourself! He has too many other things
to attend to, like world peace. I'm sure God does not have time
to answer the pointless prayers of . . ."

Todd put his first two fingers in his mouth and, facing the
opening of the inlet, let loose with a whistle so shrill that Christy

covered her ears. "It's a Wave Rider," he announced. "Help me flag it down, Christy."

Christy stumbled quickly to the back of the boat and slipped off her life vest, ready to wave it in the air.

"You can't be sure they're coming this way," Marti muttered, remaining in her seat but craning her neck.

They could all hear the high-pitched roar of the jet ski now, and it definitely was coming their way. Christy began yelling along with Todd's whistling. The minute the Wave Rider came into view, Christy waved the life vest over her head, and Todd waved his arms.

Just as quickly as the Wave Rider came into view, it shot past the cove and disappeared.

"What did I tell you?" Marti said. "Why don't you ever listen to me?"

"I think it's coming back," Christy said, straining to hear any change in the sound of the Wave Rider's motor.

"You're right," Todd said. "Get ready to wave your vest again." Before he finished speaking, the Wave Rider appeared and made a quick turn into their secret cove. The driver, a girl with long, dark hair, wearing a bright pink life vest, cut the engine and floated over to the boat. She had a dark tan, the color of chocolate cinnamon, and a white smile like a crescent moon.

"Need help?" the girl called out.

"Ran out of gas," Todd answered. "Can you give me a lift to the marina?"

"Sure. Hop on."

"Make sure your aunt stays here," Todd said to Christy. "I'll be right back."

"I heard that!" Marti said. "Of course I'm going to stay here. Where do you think I'd go? Just don't be getting any ideas in your head that this young girl is an answer to your prayers."

"You prayed for help?" the girl asked.

"Yep," Todd said, sliding into the water and swimming over to the Wave Rider.

"Are you by any chance a Christian?" the girl questioned.

"Christy and I both are," Todd said.

"This is so cool!" the girl said excitedly. "I'm Natalie. I'm a Christian, too! And you're not going to believe this, but I actually came down to this part of the lake because something inside kept kind of nudging me to go this way, you know what I mean?"

"Oh, this is ridiculous," Marti spouted, slouching back in her seat.

Christy felt like laughing at her aunt's refusal to believe in answered prayer even when she saw it with her own eyes. She knew it wasn't funny, but why couldn't her aunt see God had responded to their request for help?

Todd positioned himself on the back of the Wave Rider, and he and Natalie waved and took off, leaving Christy alone with her aunt. She waited a few minutes before trying to start a conversation.

"Why is it so hard for you to believe in God, Aunt Marti?"

"I believe in God."

"I mean, to surrender your life to Him and ask Jesus to be your Savior?"

"I refuse to get into a religious discussion with you, Christina. You are far too young to understand such things."

Christy hushed up. All she could think was, *I'm glad Jesus didn't consider me too young when I gave Him my heart.*

Todd and Natalie returned in less than an hour, and the boat started right up. "Thanks!" Todd called out, waving to Natalie as she took off. He slowly directed the boat out of the inlet but cranked it into high gear as soon as he hit the open lake.

"Slow down!" Marti squawked. "It's too cold! You're going to miss the houseboat if you go too fast."

Todd slowed a little and told Christy, "Keep looking for the houseboat. They could be anywhere along this part of the shore."

It really was chilly, with the wind off the lake and the late afternoon sun hanging low in the sky. The sun looked so much different from the one that had greeted Christy and Todd at daybreak. This big, sinking orange ball looked tired and ready for a rest, and so did Christy.

They finally found the houseboat after several trips in and out of a variety of coves along the shoreline. Katie was fishing off the roof, and Bob and Doug sat on the back deck, deliberating over a game of chess.

"They're here," Katie called out. "Finally! Where have you guys been?"

Christy noticed that another houseboat was parked across the cove from them. Katie yelled so loudly Christy felt sure the people in the other houseboat must be ready to come out on their deck to find out what all the commotion was about. Todd docked the boat, but before he or Christy had a chance to explain why they were gone so long, Marti started in.

"It was absolutely horrible," she moaned to Bob, who offered her a hand out of the boat. "We were shipwrecked for hours! I'm frozen to the bone!"

"We ran out of gas," Todd explained to the curious eyes that looked to him for an explanation. "We prayed, and God sent an angel on a Wave Rider."

"Why don't you come on in and take a warm shower," Bob suggested. "Everything is ready for dinner except the steaks, and the coals are perfect, so I'll slap 'em on the grill. You got back just in time.''

Christy gladly took Bob's suggestion to hop in the shower. She was surprised at how nice the shower was in the houseboat, and they had plenty of hot water. There was even a place to plug in her hair dryer. She took her time drying and combing out her hair. Better to finish that in the bathroom than to fling her wet hair all over her aunt again.

As it turned out, Christy didn't have much to worry about. Marti didn't emerge from her room for the rest of the night. Bob, the ever-patient and loving husband, prepared her dinner and took it to her.

Christy felt fresh after her shower and only slightly ruffled from the day's adventure. She slipped into a pair of jeans, a favorite cream-colored knit sweater, and a pair of weathered white tennis shoes. The water from the shower made her hair especially soft, not frizzy like the water at home in Escondido. She could feel a little bit of sunburn on her cheeks and thought how rosy and cheerful it made her look.

Quickly dabbing on some mascara and going over her lips a second time with a tube of clear lip gloss, Christy took another look in the mirror. She felt pretty. Pretty in an outdoors, healthy, glowing sort of way. She wondered if Todd would notice.

Just then Katie knocked on the door and said, ''Are you coming, Christy? The steaks are almost ready.''

Christy opened the door and pulled her friend inside. ''Well?'' Christy whispered. ''How did it go with Doug this afternoon?''

''What do you mean, 'how did it go?' How was it supposed to go?''

''I thought you guys might start to, you know . . . get together, sort of, if you had some time alone.''

"Christy, what makes you think Doug is at all interested in me?" Katie's words came out almost sad.

"I think you two would be perfect for each other. He's a great guy. It would help if you would show him a little more attention. Let him know that you like him."

"And what makes you think I like him?" Katie asked.

"Why wouldn't you? He's tall, good-looking, athletic, a super-strong Christian, and a lot of fun to be around. I'm sure he likes you."

"Then he'd be the first guy ever," Katie said dryly.

"And what a great first guy!" Christy tried to cheer her friend on. "Come on, Katie. You've got to emotionally walk away from all those bad memories of Rick, and who was that missionary kid from Ecuador? Glen? It's time to move on."

"You're probably right." Katie glanced in the mirror and noticed that her freckled nose was sunburned. "Oh, no, now I'm going to peel."

Christy looked in the mirror. The contrast between the two girls was evident. Katie's fair skin, green eyes, and copper-colored hair made her look young, almost childish. Christy's tan made her blue-green eyes stand out. Her smooth skin looked flawless next to Katie's freckles, and her clean hair looked silky compared to Katie's unbrushed hair.

"How can I compete with that?" Katie asked, motioning to their reflections and focusing on Christy.

"We're not competing, Katie. This is not some sport. Besides, if it were, you'd whomp me hands down. This is just the guys, and I'm with Todd, so why don't you see what you can do about getting together with Doug?"

It surprised Christy to hear herself talking like that. She had never pushed Katie toward any guy before. She knew her motive was to get Katie and Doug together so she wouldn't have to feel awkward around Doug.

"Ladies," Bob's voice called through the closed bathroom door, "we're about to sit down to dinner, and we have a guest. Care to join us?"

"We'll be right there," Christy called back. "Is there any way I can encourage you by telling you you're wonderful just the way you are, and you're adorable, and any guy would be crazy not to see how terrific you are?"

"Do you really think so?" Katie asked.

"Yes, I really think so. And I think Doug would definitely be interested in you if you showed some interest in him."

"You sure?"

Christy nodded. "Come on, let's go out there and see what happens."

"Okay," Katie said, smoothing back her hair before opening the door. "Here goes nothing."

The two girls walked side by side down the short hallway to the kitchen. What they saw made them suddenly stop and stare.

CHAPTER FOUR

Try, Try Again

Todd was standing next to the table with his arm around a stunning young girl. She looked as though she couldn't be much older than fourteen, but her figure made her look more mature. Her dark hair was pulled back by her sunglasses and her lips curled in a charming crescent-moon smile, revealing perfect white teeth set off by her deep, chocolate cinnamon skin.

"Christy," Todd said, "guess who's in the houseboat across the cove from us?"

"Natalie," Christy said, forcing a friendly smile, "what a surprise!"

Katie poked Christy in the side as if to silently ask, "And who is Natalie?"

"Katie, this is Natalie. Natalie is the one who rescued us this afternoon."

Todd moved his arm from Natalie's shoulders and was about to say something when Doug came in from the side of the houseboat with a platter of barbecued steaks in his hand. He apparently hadn't seen Natalie arrive.

"Hi!" Doug said brightly, his grin dancing across his face. Doug looked to Todd for an explanation.

"This is Natalie. Our angel on the Wave Rider."

Natalie giggled. It was a cute, innocent giggle. What was it Todd had said about how irresistible innocent girls were?

"Would you like to join us for dinner?" Doug offered. "We have plenty."

"We already ate," Natalie said. "I just happened to notice it was your boat parked over here so I thought I'd come say hi."

"This is awesome," Doug said. "We're going to have a campfire on the beach after dinner; you'll join us, won't you?"

"I guess. Sure. Thanks for asking."

Then, as if someone had said to Katie, "Let the games begin," she jumped into the conversation. Gaining Doug's attention obviously was her goal. "Those steaks look great, Doug. Did you cook them? I bet you guys are hungry. I sure am. We should sit down to dinner, don't you think?"

Bob, who had been observing all this from the kitchen sink where he was pouring a pan of hot peas into a serving bowl, joined Katie's team. "Good idea. Let's sit down."

"I'll let myself out," Natalie said softly. "I guess I'll watch for your campfire later on."

"Don't leave," Doug said, sliding onto the vinyl bench seat and patting the spot next to him. "There's plenty of room, Natalie. Come sit by me."

Katie took the challenge and bolted to the table where she slid in on Doug's other side. "Are you as hungry as I am?" Katie asked Doug, looking for an answer from him.

Christy found herself a chair and pulled it up to the table. She wasn't sure how she felt about what was going on here. In a way she was glad Katie was flirting a little with Doug. Maybe all Katie needed was the competitive factor that Natalie brought into the situation. Still, Natalie had to be several years younger than Katie and Christy. If she were about fourteen, that would make Natalie eight years younger than Doug. Surely he knew that. He wasn't really flirting with her, was he?

Throughout dinner Natalie giggled at all of Doug's comments, and Katie popped off with some of her classic lines at the right moments. Christy wondered if Todd had any clue as to what was going on.

Do guys ever? she thought.

After dinner Christy helped Bob with the dishes. Todd and Doug, followed by Katie and Natalie, took off to start the campfire.

"I brought some marshmallows," Bob offered, handing a bag to Christy after the dishes were done. "Some coat hangers are in the hall closet. Why don't you join the others?"

Christy went in search of the coat hangers and glanced toward the shore out the window. The fire was already glowing. In the darkness she could make out Doug's frame with both girls on either side of him, in the exact spots they had occupied at dinner.

Natalie seemed like a sweet girl, and it was fun to meet another Christian and to have been rescued by her. Christy just hoped that, being so young and vulnerable, Natalie wouldn't misinterpret Doug's attention. Even more than that, Christy hoped Katie wouldn't get hurt, especially after Christy's big pep talk with her.

Did I do the right thing, pushing Katie toward Doug like that?

Armed with marshmallows and five coat hangers, Christy grabbed a beach towel and headed for the campfire. She spread her towel on the smooth rocks next to Todd and asked, "Anyone ready for a marshmallow?"

Doug didn't hear her. Katie had him tangled up in a thumb wrestling contest.

"I'd like one," Natalie said, leaving her post next to Doug and joining Christy. As she skewered the white puff, Natalie looked past Christy and said to Todd, "I still can't believe you guys are all Christians. That is so cool!!"

Todd, Christy, and Natalie chatted, quietly roasting marshmallows while Doug and Katie continued their contest. When they seemed to have had enough thumb wrestling, Doug and Katie joined the other three and started another competition. This time it was to see who could get his or her marshmallow the brownest without burning it.

After three marshmallows, Christy was full of the sticky sugar and placed her coat hanger against one of the large rocks lining the fire pit. As she let go of the hanger, Todd stretched out his hand.

She thought he was reaching for her coat hanger, but instead he grasped her hand and wrapped his thick, warm fingers around hers. She turned to him and smiled. Todd smiled back. They were together, sitting close under a star-filled sky, holding hands. This was what Christy had always dreamed going together would be like. She moved a little closer to Todd so their hands could rest comfortably on his folded leg.

That's when she noticed Natalie looking at them, and Christy realized how awkward Natalie must feel with two college guys paying all their attention to Katie and Christy while Natalie sat alone like a leftover. Christy remembered how explosive her emotions were when she was fourteen, and she tried to draw Natalie into a conversation. Even though Todd and Christy were sitting close and holding hands, Christy thought it didn't have to mean they excluded Natalie.

Doug and Katie continued their marshmallow competition until the entire bag had been devoured. During their contest Na-

talie and Christy talked about school, family, and church. When
the topic of Jet Skiing came up, Doug sat down next to Natalie
with a string of questions.

Now it was Katie's turn to look like the leftover. The more
Doug and Natalie talked, the more Katie seemed to withdraw.
When Natalie asked Doug if he wanted to try out her Wave Rider
tomorrow morning, Doug lit up with excitement and gave Natalie
one of his hugs.

Christy wondered how Natalie would interpret Doug's affec-
tionate expression. She seemed to glow a little brighter in the
dwindling firelight as the two of them made their morning plans.
There was no problem trying to guess how Katie took Doug's gesture toward Natalie. Katie excused herself from the group and
walked back to the houseboat.

Instinctively Christy wanted to rush to her friend's side and
comfort her. Still, she didn't want to leave Todd and the warmth
of his hand encircling hers. Even though Christy knew it was
probably not the best decision, she let Katie go off by herself.

"You think she's okay?" Todd asked.

"I think so. It's been a long day for everyone," Christy said.

After all, Christy told herself, *Katie should be old enough to handle
these kinds of disappointments on her own without always having me
there to cheer her up. She'll meet a nice guy someday who will appreciate
her*.

Christy tried to convince herself it wasn't her fault Doug
didn't seem to be as interested in Katie as Christy had hoped he
would be. Doug and Katie had been around each other before at
get-togethers, but somehow Christy had imagined this would be
the trip that would draw the two of them together the way she
and Todd were finally together.

Oh well, Christy thought with a sigh, *I guess it wasn't meant to be. Certainly Katie can see that. She'll snap out of it by morning.*

Christy's prediction was wrong. Katie didn't snap out of it. Christy lingered in bed, hoping to talk to Katie when she woke up, but Katie pretended to be still asleep.

"I don't know what to do," Christy confided to Uncle Bob at the breakfast table where only the two of them sat. "I think Katie's not just hurt because Doug didn't pay much attention to her last night, but I think she's mad at me for even suggesting she flirt with him."

It was easy for Christy to pour her heart out to her uncle. This morning she did it as if the confession would release her from the guilt she felt for pushing Katie into something she wasn't convinced she should do.

"You can't do anything," Bob said. "You tried to do something yesterday by coaxing her toward Doug, and that didn't work out. There's not much you can do or say at this point until her feelings mend some. It'll happen. It just takes time. Until then, leave her alone."

Then with a smile and a sip of his coffee, Bob added, "Trust me. When it comes to advice on women getting over being mad at you, I'm talking from experience." He gingerly nodded toward the closed bedroom door down the hall, where Christy could hear her aunt humming as she got ready for the day. Apparently Bob had taken his own advice and had allowed his wife time to be alone last night so she could mend from the trauma of the previous day.

Marti emerged bright and smiling, ready for a fresh start. "Good morning, you two. Beautiful day, isn't it? I thought we could all relax a little today. Take it easy, soak up some sun. What do you think? Are we all ready to enjoy ourselves?"

Christy thought her aunt was a little too perky, but she preferred perky over sulky any day. Besides, she agreed with Marti's advice on taking it easy. Maybe that would be the best thing for Katie and Doug, too.

For two sun-drenched, gentle hours, Christy sat by Todd's side on the top of the houseboat, reading while he fished. It was wonderful to be together without feeling they had to be doing or saying something to fill the time. Todd caught two medium-sized trout, which he cleaned while Christy watched.

Meanwhile Katie was off by herself, swimming for a little while, then kicking back on the deck while Bob and Doug worked on the rudder. Bob thought it needed some attention, so he had Doug in the water while he gave directions from the boat.

"Why don't we fry your fish for lunch?" Marti suggested once Todd had them cleaned.

"There's only enough for about one bite per person," Todd said.

"That's okay. It's all part of the experience of being on the river, don't you think?"

They were really on a lake, not a river, but no one mentioned this to Marti. It was nice to have her in a good mood.

You really can be a sweetie when you want to be, can't you, Aunt Marti? Now if only Katie would perk up a little, Doug could see what a sweetie she can be.

"Who's up for some water skiing?" Bob asked after lunch. "The rudder is as good as new. Katie? You want to go out with me?"

Katie gave him a wry smile and said, "I guess I'd better take you up on the offer. You may be the only male who ever asks me to go out with him."

Bob gave Katie a friendly hug and said, "I want to see you up on one ski again. You're very good, you know."

Katie shrugged. Christy interpreted the gesture to mean Katie would give up her athletic ability in a second if it meant a guy would be interested in her.

"You coming too, Christy?" Bob asked. "Or how about you guys? I made sure the tank is full, Todd."

"Good thinking," Todd said. "Sure, I'll go."

"How about you, Doug?" Bob asked, sounding like a coach trying to get all the cool guys to sign up for his team.

"Actually, I told Natalie I'd go out on the Wave Rider with her at two." Doug looked a little sheepish. "I'll stick around here. You guys go have fun. Maybe I'll see you out there."

When Christy, Bob, Todd, and Katie headed out for a good skiing spot, the awkwardness Christy felt with Doug the day before returned, only this time it was with Katie. She could feel her best friend's snubbing as if it were a chill wind.

Why is it that everything started to go bad with all my friends the minute Todd and I started to go together? Is there some unwritten rule that once you have a boyfriend everyone else is commanded to turn against you?

What hurt Christy the most was that she had been so eager to talk to Katie about Todd and how they had decided they would go together. Now that was the last thing Katie wanted to hear.

"Hit it!" Katie called from her position in the water sometime later. It was the last run of the day, and Christy had spent the afternoon mulling over her thoughts while she held up the ski flag whenever Todd, Bob, or Katie had gone down in the water.

"Do you want to try after Katie's run?" Bob asked Christy. "It looks as though we'll be leaving fairly early in the morning, so this may be your last chance."

Christy thought of the pep talk she had given herself after her last attempt at water skiing and decided she needed to give it one more try.

After Katie successfully completed a perfect run, she let go of the tow rope and dropped into the water. She seemed surprised to see Christy coming into the water.

"You're not going to try skiing again, are you?" Katie asked.

"I think I need to give it one more sincere effort before giving up," Christy said, trying hard to sound confident.

Katie shrugged, climbed back into the boat, and tossed Christy the rope. Don't you want these skis?" Katie asked, holding up the two skis while Christy struggled in the water to fit both her feet into the single ski.

"No, I think I'll try this one."

"Most people learn how to ski on two before they try one," Katie reasoned.

"Well," Christy said, feeling foolish and noble at the same time, "I guess I'm not like most people."

She positioned the ski toward the boat, tightly gripped the tow rope, and tried to remember everything Todd had told her. Then she bellowed, "Hit it!"

The rope edged across the face of the water as the boat pulled it taut. The instant she felt its tug, Christy began to lean back and let the boat do the work. The ski seemed to bounce and wiggle, making it difficult for her to find her balance. Then it happened. Miracle of miracles, she was standing up! She was skiing. And on one ski, no less.

"All right, Christy!" she could hear Todd cheering.

The boat slowly turned to the right. It was just enough of a shift to make her lose her balance. Christy wobbled and then tumbled into the water.

She must have been up on the ski for forty seconds, but to

hear Todd tell Doug back at the houseboat, it sounded as though Christy had broken a world record. Maybe it was, for her. Maybe she was, as Katie had said, "athletically impaired," but at least she had tried. And in that effort she had experienced enough achievement to make her feel like an Olympic medalist.

Christy was the first to shower and change while the guys secured the boat. Bob had decided they needed to camp closer to the marina that night so they could get an earlier start in the morning for their long ride home.

"I heard you experienced a great success this afternoon," Marti said when Christy emerged from the bathroom.

"It was a pretty big deal for me," Christy admitted. "But you should have seen Katie. She's incredible on skis!" Christy flashed a smile at Katie, who was helping to get dinner ready. Christy hoped it might mend some of the holes in their communication line.

Katie took the compliment and looked over her shoulder at Christy. It was the first time their eyes had really met all day. "You inspired me, Christy, to keep trying at the things that don't come easily for me."

"I can't imagine there would be very many things that don't come easily for you, dear," Marti said.

"Guys don't come easily for me. Particularly guys like Doug."

"Why didn't you say so?" Marti asked. "How silly of me not to have noticed! Well, if you're serious about taking Christy's inspiration to keep trying, then I have a plan."

Marti motioned for the two girls to come closer so she could fill them in on her scheme. Marti whispered, pointed outside, looked at her watch, and then gave Katie strict instructions to take a shower and not to come out "until you look and feel as pretty as a picture."

It was an ironic analogy for Katie, who worked for a photographer and often told Christy the secret touch-ups used on all the best pictures in the shop. Christy thought maybe Marti would be just the right touch-up artist to get things going between Katie and Doug.

Perhaps the best part was that Katie was willing to try. It made Christy feel as if they were being drawn back together as friends to work on Marti's project.

Christy noticed that the water Katie had started on the stove was boiling, so she added the measuring cup of rice, put on the lid, and turned the flame down low.

"Now, the chicken is already in the oven. It looks like we need to get this salad going," Marti said. "I'll have Bob set up the card table on the back deck."

Marti busied herself with her dinner arrangements while Christy made the salad and watched Todd and Doug out the window. They both had dark tans after a summer of endless surfing and looked relaxed in their T-shirts and swim trunks, helping Bob tie up the boat. Marti joined them and gave firm instructions on what time they were to be ready for dinner and how they were to look and smell when they showed.

Christy sprinkled a bag of croutons on top of her finished salad and smiled at her determined aunt. With Marti back in her "cruise director" mode, there was no telling how their dinner might turn out.

CHAPTER FIVE

Moonlight and Noses

"We need one more chair," Marti instructed.

Christy pulled the last folding chair from the closet and carried it to the back deck, where Marti stood by the card table. Not just any card table. This table had been transformed into an elegant dining spot for Todd, Christy, Doug, and Katie, complete with tablecloth, candles, and Marti's handsome name cards at each place. This was all part of her surefire plan to bring Doug and Katie together, a romantic sunset dinner on a floating restaurant.

"There," Marti said, tucking the last chair into its spot. "The boys should be done with their showers soon. Where's Katie? You two lovely young ladies should be standing out here by the deck, casually waiting for them to arrive. And remember, neither of you is to sit down until the boys pull out the chairs for you."

Christy nodded at all her aunt's "charm school" instructions. She had to admit, this was fun.

"How does this look?" Katie asked, stepping out on the deck wearing an oversized white T-shirt and shorts.

"Oh my!" Marti said, looking concerned. "Is that the best you can do?"

"Well, this was originally an invitation to go houseboating, not to the prom," Katie said sarcastically. "I would have brought my black sequined evening gown with matching gloves and mink stole, if you would have told me."

Christy glanced down at her own jeans shorts and the rolled-up, long-sleeved denim shirt with a torn pocket. *I wonder why Aunt Marti didn't criticize my outfit? Does she think a person only has to look good when she's trying to get a boyfriend?*

"Let's do this," Marti said, fussing with the long ends of Katie's T-shirt and tying them into a knot at her right hip. "Much more flattering. Shows off your flat stomach."

Katie laughed, startling Marti. "Thanks for the tip, but I'm not much of a knot-on-the-hip type of person." Katie untied it and let the now-wrinkled shirt hang naturally. "I did put on some makeup. Did anyone notice?"

In the dimming light of the evening sky, Christy hadn't. She and Marti both moved in closer to examine the makeup. It was hard to tell, but in a subtle way Katie's green eyes looked larger and more sparkling.

"There's always your personality," Marti said, stepping back and giving Katie another up-and-down scan. "You have a wonderful personality. Use it to your advantage, dear."

Then excusing herself to find the boys, Marti waltzed past Christy and Katie and into the bright lights of the houseboat kitchen.

" 'Use your personality, dear,' " Katie mimicked. "I think I just got slammed big time. What do you think?"

"I think we should both relax a little here and enjoy my aunt's game of Enchanted Evening. What do you think?"

"I think . . ." Katie hesitated. "Never mind what I think. You're right. This could be a lot of fun. Just the four of us. No unexpected 'angels' dropping by, I hope.''

"I don't think so. Natalie's houseboat pulled out while you were in the shower.''

"So we just stand here and act casual until the guys show up?''

Just then the motor to the houseboat started, and Bob began to maneuver their way out of the cove and into the main part of the lake.

"What's going on?" Katie asked.

"My uncle wanted to be closer to the marina so we can check in earlier in the morning. Aunt Marti is going to serve our dinners while Bob floats our restaurant under the stars. Pretty fun, don't you think?''

Katie started to brighten up a little. "Yeah, I guess this could be kind of fun. It'd be even more fun if I didn't feel like such a fashion degenerate.''

Christy laughed. "You look fine. Look at me, though; I'm the slob of the year!''

"Hardly. You always look cute. Even in grubbies you look cute. How do you do that?''

"Do what? I don't do anything.''

"That's what I mean," Katie said. "You're one of those people who looks good in anything.''

Before Christy had a chance to return a compliment to her insecure friend, the guys entered the kitchen, filling the compact area with their presence. They immediately evoked Marti's laughter.

"What's so funny in there?" Katie asked, trying to peer through the mesh in the screen door.

The guys turned toward them and headed for the back deck. Apparently they had taken Marti's grooming threats to heart. Both guys had parted their hair in the middle and watered it down so that it stuck to their heads. They both had on T-shirts and shorts, but they had constructed bow ties out of paper towels and had somehow fastened them to their T-shirts at the neckline.

"Come meet your dates," Marti said with hints of laughter still tickling her voice. "Right this way, gentlemen."

Marti ushered them out to the deck, where Katie and Christy stood waiting. The guys smiled, and Christy noticed something dark on Doug's upper lip.

"Good evening," Doug greeted them, twitching his face a little and drawing attention to his painted-on moustache. "I'd like to thank whichever one of you left your mascara in the bathroom. I found it very useful."

They all laughed. Todd pulled out his chair and sat down. Doug followed his example. Under Marti's firm glare, Katie and Christy remained standing, waiting for the guys to pull out their chairs.

"Oh, I beg your pardon, miss," Doug said, catching on before Todd and rising to pull out Katie's chair. "May I?"

Katie graciously lowered herself into the folding chair and played right along. "Oh, thank you ever so much, kind sir. There's nothing like a man with a moustache to add that festive touch to any occasion."

"That's me," Doug said, pretending to twirl his moustache, "the man with the festive touch."

Todd pulled out Christy's chair, and Marti said, "Please make yourselves comfortable. Your salads are before you, and I shall return momentarily with a basket of bread sticks."

The houseboat slowly motored across the lake as the sun slid behind the hills. A gentle evening breeze rose from off the water.

"Look over there," Todd said, pointing to the hills to the left. As they watched, the moon rose like a prize-winning harvest pumpkin and lit their table the way a paper lantern lights up a garden party.

"Awesome," Doug said.

"Isn't it beautiful?" Katie asked. "What a perfect night. A *'bella notte,'* as they say. All we need is spaghetti and meatballs and a couple of Italian waiters to sing to us."

"Why?" Doug asked.

"Because it feels like the night in that movie when the dogs are eating spaghetti, and the boy dog uses his nose to push the last meatball over to the girl dog."

"Why didn't you say so?" Doug asked, playfully using his nose to nudge the cherry tomato from his salad off his plate and toward Katie. The tomato made it about halfway to Katie's plate before it toppled over the side of the card table and hit the deck with a splat.

"Now we know why they used a meatball in the movie," Doug said dryly.

They all laughed, and Christy felt happy. Very happy. She wondered if Todd were enjoying all this as much as she was. He looked downright silly with his slicked-back hair and paper towel bow tie. She would expect this kind of goofing off from Doug. It was a nice surprise to see Todd acting a little crazy.

Just one more reason to like him so much, Christy thought. *I wonder if Todd enjoys being around me as much as I enjoy being with him? The way Doug is teasing Katie, I wonder if he's starting to get more interested in her?*

Todd prayed for their food, and they dug in, chatting and dining under the moon. Marti appeared right on cue with two dinner plates steaming with the main course of rice, broccoli, and chicken with some kind of lemon-butter sauce and sprinkled with slivered almonds. Marti served Christy and Katie first and then returned with two plates for the guys.

"Is everything to your liking?" Marti asked.

"Great," Todd said.

Christy thought it looked great except for the nuts. She hated nuts. She'd tried some in the past and had thought they were okay. But now she was back to disliking them. Maybe no one would notice if she discretely scraped off the almonds and pushed them to the side of her plate.

"Do you happen to have any meatballs?" Doug asked. Christy could tell Marti was a little perturbed that they were being so silly and not acting mature and romantic as she had planned.

"I'm going to put some music on these outside speakers," Marti announced. "Some soothing, evening dinner music to help set the mood for you young people."

A few moments later, the strains of sweet violins surrounded them.

Katie burst out laughing. "It's the Italian music we ordered!"

"I like it," Christy said, quickly defending the classical music.

"Are you serious?" Katie asked.

"Of course I'm serious. I love this kind of music. Don't you?"

"Sure, in an elevator or at the dentist's office!"

"I like it," Todd said, reaching over and giving Christy's arm a tender squeeze. "This is music to touch the heart." He smiled at Christy, and she smiled back.

"Do you kind of get the feeling these two might want to be alone?" Katie said to Doug. "We could always take our dinner plates up on the roof. What do you think?"

Doug seemed to have sobered quickly after all the laughter. Instead of answering Katie, he lifted another bite of chicken to his mouth and said, "Good dinner."

"I made the rice," Katie said. "Well, actually I boiled the water."

No one seemed to think that was as funny as Katie did. They ate quietly, aware of Marti's ever-watchful gaze on them. She seemed pleased that the music had apparently tempered their silliness, and she tiptoed in and out as she served dessert.

The quiet must have been too much for Katie, because when the brownie with a cloud of whipped cream on top was served to Doug, Christy spotted a mischievous glint in her friend's eye.

"Eww," Katie said, looking at Doug's dessert and then at hers. "Can you smell that?"

"What?" Doug asked.

Katie daintily sniffed at her whipped cream. "I don't think we should eat this. Can't you smell it?"

"Smell what?" Doug said, sniffing his dessert. "I don't smell anything."

"Then smell mine," Katie said. She lifted her dessert plate with one hand on the bottom and held it up for Doug to smell. Doug leaned forward. Then Katie let loose with her sweet revenge and shoved the whipped cream and brownie into Doug's unsuspecting face.

"Gotcha!" Katie squealed with delight as Doug peeled the goo off his face. "That's for flipping Christy and me off the raft the first day. Now we're even."

Doug licked at the whipped cream and felt the table in search of his napkin.

"Here you go," Todd said, removing his bow tie and offering it to Doug. "I knew these things would come in handy."

Katie was still laughing. Marti hurried outside to see what was going on. "What happened here? How did this happen?"

"Just a little accident," Doug said good-naturedly. Half of his pretend mustache had been wiped off by Todd's bow tie. The other half of his face still sported chunks of chocolate and whipped cream. "Could we order one more dessert and maybe a few paper towels out here?"

Katie had dropped her fork during her attack, and as she bent down to pick it up, Doug lifted his empty plate to hand it to Marti. Somehow, the moment Katie's head came up, Doug's long arm swung out, connecting with Katie's face. The plate and his hand slammed into Katie's nose. The plate crashed to the ground, and Katie let out a wail and grabbed her nose. Christy sprang from her chair.

Doug, still wearing his dessert, jumped up and frantically said, "I didn't mean that, Katie. It was an accident. Really. Are you okay? You guys, tell her it was an accident!"

Katie seemed to be trying not to cry, but the tears came and so did a gush of blood from her nose.

"Don't tilt your head back," Todd said, jumping up and grabbing a corner of the tablecloth to apply to Katie's nose. "Here, put your hand on this and press right here."

Christy stepped back and let Todd take over. The sight of blood on Katie's white T-shirt made Christy feel kind of woozy. It all had happened so fast. The classical music still played in the background in cruel contrast to the frenzied activity around the table.

"Don't hold your breath," Todd said, his voice calm and steady. "Try to breathe normally through your mouth. Christy, could you bring me some ice in a plastic bag?"

"Sure," Christy sprang into action and slid past her aunt, who seemed to be frozen in place next to the screen door. Christy grabbed a plastic bag from the cupboard and filled it with ice cubes. She was glad Todd knew what to do. He had probably seen lots of bloody noses during his years of surfing.

"Everything okay back there?" Bob called from the captain's seat at the front of the boat.

"Nothing major," Christy called down the hallway. "Katie got a bloody nose. It's under control, I think." She slipped out to the deck and handed the bag of ice to Todd. "Can I do anything else?"

"No, thanks. This ought to do it. Hold this ice right here, Katie, with one hand. Good. Now give me your other hand." Todd guided her finger to a pressure point on the gum under her top lip. "Press here. That's good. It should stop bleeding in a minute."

Todd was right. Within a few minutes the crisis had passed. Doug wiped the rest of the brownie off his face and said, "Hey, it was totally an accident, Katie. Honest. I didn't see you there."

Katie said in a garbled voice, "That's probably because you had brownies in your eyes."

Everyone let out a short, relieved spurt of laughter. Everyone but Marti. She seemed completely undone. They had ruined her plans for a perfect evening.

"Do you want to share my dessert?" Christy asked, not sure what to say to Katie.

"I'm not exactly hungry anymore," Katie said, wiping her cheek. "I think I'd better go change."

Even though no one told them to clear the table, the three remaining dinner guests started to gather up the dishes and tear down the romantic dinner for four. The moon was now high above them as Christy blew out the candles and wadded up the soiled tablecloth.

The *bella notte* had not exactly turned out the way she had hoped.

CHAPTER SIX

Michael and Fred

"No, it's me," Katie whispered to Christy in the darkness. "I know it is."

"No, it's not," Christy immediately responded. "It's the circumstances, or the guys, but really, Katie, it's not you."

The two of them had traded sleeping quarters with the guys for their final night of the trip and were lying in their sleeping bags on the roof of the houseboat. Nothing was above them but the inky sky flung with thousands of diamonds. The moon had taken its curtain call for the night and slipped behind Mount Shasta.

"I know you're saying all this to be nice to me, Christy, but I'd like to think our friendship is past the point of us lying to each other in the interest of being polite."

"I'm not lying. You don't have a boyfriend, not because of anything you're doing or not doing. The right guy hasn't come along yet. That's all."

"In almost eighteen years not one 'right guy' has come along, and you think it's *not* because of me? Think again."

It was silent for a few minutes except for the lulling sound of the water lapping on the houseboat's sides and a few late-night crickets and frogs saying good night to each other.

"Maybe we should pray about it," Christy suggested meekly.

"You mean the way you pray for your future husband and have a shoe box full of letters to him stashed under your bed? I don't think so, Christy. That's not me. I could never write a letter to someone I don't know. And what am I supposed to pray? 'God, bring me a man—now'? I thought really spiritual Christians prayed for patience and stuff like that. Not for boyfriends."

"But, Katie, if God knows all about us and if He cares about everything that happens to us, then of course you should pray about everything. Even about a boyfriend. God already knows what would be best for you, too."

"I hope you know how easy it is for you to say all that," Katie said quickly. "You have *the* perfect boyfriend of the universe. Of course you believe God is giving you His best. It's harder to believe stuff like that when you're like me and no answer to your prayers is sitting next to you holding your hand. I mean, what if God's best for me is that I don't get a boyfriend?"

"God still cares, Katie."

"How do you know that? I mean, don't you wonder sometimes how much of what we believe about God is real and how much of it we say simply because we want to believe it?"

Christy propped herself up on her elbow and looked at Katie. "What do you mean? It sounds as if you're saying you don't trust God."

"I don't know. It just seems God has forgotten about me when it comes to boyfriends, that's all. Not that I hold it against Him. After all, God must be rather busy these days—earthquakes, pestilence, famines, wars. What's a plea from Katie for a boyfriend when He has so much else to tend to?"

"God is big enough to handle all that and your feelings, too.

Please don't think He's forgotten you."

"If you say so," Katie said with a sigh.

It was quiet for a few moments before Katie asked, "So what time are we leaving in the morning?"

"I don't know," Christy said. "Pretty early, I guess. I'm sure the rest of them will wake us when they get up."

"Then we'd better get some sleep. Good night." Katie rolled over on her side with her back to Christy. In minutes, the only sound that came from her was the deep, slow, rhythmic breathing of someone lost in dreamland.

Christy was unable to enter dreamland herself for quite some time. She lay on her back in the stillness, watching for shooting stars and thinking about Katie. It bothered her that Katie had sounded as though she were doubting her faith in God. What bothered Christy even more was that she didn't have any really good answers for Katie.

Not that I have to defend You, God. You are God. You can do what You want. But I do wish sometimes that You and Your ways were easier to understand. Sometimes all I know is that You're there. Maybe sometimes that's all I need to know.

Christy noticed a trail of thin, iridescent clouds moving slowly across the night sky. *The dust beneath His feet*, she thought. *You are here, and You do care, don't You, God? Please help Katie to see that and to understand You.* Christy closed her eyes and drifted into a deep, sweet sleep.

When she awoke, the first thing Christy saw was Katie's face, which made Christy gasp. Katie had two black rings around both her eyes, a result of the blow she took to her nose the night before.

"Katie," Christy called softly, nudging her on the shoulder. "Katie, wake up."

"What?" Katie answered, sounding groggy and irritated.

"Just five more minutes, okay?"

"It's time to get up, Katie. We're on the houseboat. We have to get going. And you need to look in a mirror." Christy said the last part in a low voice and bit her lower lip, wondering how Katie would react to what she would see in the mirror.

Christy knew that if it had happened to her, she would be devastated and would probably try to find a way out of going to school the next morning. How could anyone begin her senior year with two black eyes?

Amazingly enough, the prize fighter look only bothered Katie for about two seconds. She looked in the mirror, screamed, then laughed and laughed until everyone else couldn't help but laugh along with her.

"You wait, Doug! I'm really going to get you back for this one!" she threatened him. She was still threatening when they arrived home from their trip late that evening. As Doug unloaded Katie's gear from the back of his truck, Katie reminded him, "When you least expect it, I *will* get you back, Doug. You can count on it."

Christy would have expected the jovial attitude to be long gone by the next morning. But when Christy picked up Katie for school, the first thing Katie said as she bounced into the car was, "What do you think of laxatives?"

Christy looked blankly at her friend. Katie had not even tried to cover up the black and blue with makeup. She looked awful. "What do you mean, laxatives?" Christy asked.

"You know the way Doug will eat anything. Why don't we make him some cookies and fill the dough with laxatives? He'd never know what hit him!"

"Katie, I can't believe you're even suggesting such a thing! That is so cruel. You would never really do anything like that, would you? You know when he hit your nose it was an accident. He felt awful about it. I think he apologized to you every five minutes on the drive home."

"Good. If you ask me, a little guilt is good for a guy."

Christy pulled into the parking lot on the back side of Kelley High and slowly proceeded up and down the rows in search of a parking place. "Did everybody decide to be early today, or what? This seems like a lot more cars than last year."

"You know how it is on the first day," Katie commented. "Everyone wants to make a good impression and all that. Besides, there are a lot more seniors this year than last. You know what I think?"

Christy found a remote parking spot and carefully eased the car in between the narrow white lines.

"I think," Katie continued, "since you're on yearbook staff you should put a picture of the parking lot in the yearbook. Nobody ever does that. I think a parking lot is as important as a locker. Maybe more so. Especially your senior year."

"You could be right. That's a good idea, Katie," Christy said, carefully locking the car and gathering the few things she had brought with her.

Even though she had been at this same school for three years and she liked Kelley High, Christy still felt as if a load of bricks had just been dumped in her stomach. It didn't matter that this was her senior year. She felt the same way she had the first day of kindergarten back in Wisconsin. Terrified.

"I think it's a really good idea," Katie chattered on cheerfully as they entered the main building. They merged into a stream of people who were all yakking and laughing and bumping each other with their backpacks slung over their shoulders. "Hey, Danny, how's it going?" Katie greeted a guy who passed them.

Danny waved back at Katie. He had on shorts and a T-shirt, and he wore sunglasses, even though he was inside the building.

"Did you see who Danny was with?" Katie said, grabbing Christy by the wrist.

The two of them looked over their shoulders at Danny and the slim, dark-haired girl he had his arm around. "That's Lynn! Can you believe they're together?" Kate said. "Actually, if you ask me, they make a good couple. I've known Danny since second grade. We used to get into trouble together when we went to Myers Middle School. I can't believe even Danny has a girl-friend!"

Christy felt relieved that Katie was by her side, breaking the ice, overshadowing Christy's timid feelings with her bold, friendly personality. Apparently first days didn't bother Katie a bit. And with two black eyes, no less!

Christy wished she had the right words at that moment to tell Katie what her friendship meant to her. How much she appreci-ated having someone beside her who could so easily lighten the brick load in her stomach.

"This is where I get off," Katie said, stopping in front of a classroom. She flashed a confident smile. "I'll see you at lunch? Same old spot?"

"Okay," Christy smiled back, trying to siphon one more burst of self-assurance from Katie before heading down the hallway to her first class. "See you!"

At 11:42 the bell rang for lunch, and Christy hurried to their meeting spot under a tree on the grass. Last year they had decided not to eat at the picnic tables or to rush out to their car and hurry through some drive-through, fast-food place like a lot of the other students did. Instead, Christy and Katie met at this remote spot.

But today their routine was interrupted. Sitting under "their" tree was a guy Christy didn't recognize. His sandaled feet were stretched out in front of him, and he looked a little too comfortable. A little too permanent. Christy stood back and watched. The guy pulled an apple from his brown leather backpack and chomped into it.

How could she tell him he was in their space?

"Hi!" Katie called out. She stepped up beside Christy and eyed the intruder.

"Who's that?" Katie said, almost loud enough for the guy to hear.

"I don't know," Christy whispered, turning back to him and scrunching up her nose at Katie. "Why don't we find a new spot?"

"Why?" Katie asked. "We can still sit there. There's more than one side to a tree, you know. Besides, once he overhears the kind of stuff we talk about, he'll probably leave in a second."

Katie boldly marched over to the tree as the guy watched. She planted herself like a flag of victory. Christy followed her lead, fully aware the guy was observing their every move.

As if nothing were out of the ordinary, Katie opened a bag of chips. "So how did all your classes go?" she asked Christy.

It was a little more difficult for Christy to jump right into their lunch routine and act as if they weren't being observed by this stranger.

Before Christy could answer, the guy spoke up. "Have you tried vitamin C?"

Christy noticed his accent. She guessed it was British.

"Excuse me?" Katie said, making eye contact with him.

"For the eyes," he said, motioning to Katie's obvious bruises. "Vitamin C with bioflavonoids three times a day. Have you tried it?" Katie looked at the guy, then at Christy. She seemed about to burst out laughing.

"Cabbage is a good source. Potatoes and tomatoes are as well."

He said 'potatoes' and 'tomatoes' funny, and Katie did start to laugh.

"Where did you come from?" she asked.

"Belfast."

Katie looked at Christy blankly. "Belfast. That's in Ireland, right?"

"Northern," the guy said quickly. "Northern Ireland. There's a vast difference, you know."

Apparently Katie and Christy didn't know. At the moment they were both captivated by this fair-skinned, dark-haired, green-eyed stranger.

"The name is Michael," the guy said, introducing himself with a smile. "And who might you be?"

"I'm Christy."

"Katie." The minute Katie said her name, Michael burst out laughing.

"What?" Katie wanted to know. "What's so funny about 'Katie'?"

"Nothing's wrong with being a Katie. It's a daft thing that I should leave a school brimming with Katies in Belfast, and the first person I meet in this California school is a Katie!"

"A 'daft thing'?" Katie repeated. The previous summer, she had started using an original expression, a "God thing," and every now and then Katie would inform Christy that Todd was doing a "Todd thing," but Katie had never heard of a "daft thing."

" 'Daft.' You know, 'daft.' You don't say that here?"

Christy and Katie both shook their heads.

"It means crazy or silly."

"Oh," both the girls said.

"So, Mike—" Katie began.

"Michael," he corrected her. "It's Michael."

"So, *Michael*," she continued, "you're giving vitamin prescriptions to a complete stranger, and you think *we're* daft? Perhaps I should tell you right up front that you're quoting vitamins to the wrong person. Unless your vitamin C with whatever-noids is found as a natural source in Twinkies, there's a pretty good chance it won't find its way into my blood system."

Michael smiled. Christy noticed that his whole face lit up when he did. He seemed harmless enough. A new guy looking to meet some people. A foreign exchange student, perhaps. Still, this friendly flirting didn't come as easily to Christy as it did to Katie.

The rest of their lunch time, Christy sat back, quietly eating her sandwich and listening to Michael and Katie's playful banter about junk food versus health food. It appeared that Michael was winning, which was a first with Katie. Christy had rarely seen a guy overpower her in any category.

"Saved by the bell," Katie said as the loud buzzer echoed across the school yard. "I haven't given up, though. I'll prove to you why my way of eating is just as good as yours."

"We'll see," Michael said with a twinkle in his eye. Pulling a piece of paper from his backpack and scanning the computer printout, he asked, "Do you happen to know where I might find room 145?"

"You're kidding!" Katie said. "That's my next class. Government with Mr. Jacobs, right?"

"I suppose I should thank my lucky stars. I'll be needing some friendly assistance when it comes to your American government." Michael slung his backpack over his arm and offered a hand to Katie to help her stand up.

"Shouldn't that be your 'Lucky Charms'? You know, that leprechaun cereal with the little colored marshmallows? Never mind," Katie said, responding to the blank look on Michael's face. "You obviously need an education in more than just American government. American breakfast cereal is a very important subject, too, I hope you know."

"Oh, is it now?"

"See you later, Christy," Katie called over her shoulder as she and Michael took off together for their class, walking close, deeply involved in their conversation.

Christy watched them for a minute before heading to her yearbook class. Michael was about the same height as Katie, and from the back, Christy could see that his thick, dark hair had reddish highlights enhanced by the sun. The back of his T-shirt had a whale on it and some kind of slogan about saving the whales. He seemed like a decent sort of guy, even though he was so different.

What am I thinking? He's a complete stranger, and he's totally captivated by Katie. This all happened too quickly. She's too eager for a boyfriend right now. How do we even know if this guy is a Christian?

Christy entered her yearbook class and felt even more uneasy. Not just about Katie, but about being with this close-knit group of students. She hadn't worked on the yearbook staff the way most of them had last year. When she sat down at a desk in the back of the room, no one even seemed to notice she was there.

Why did I ever take this class?

"Hi, Christy," a guy said, coming through the door as the bell rang.

It was Fred, the school photographer who had caught her in

several embarrassing poses last year and made sure those shots made it into the yearbook. Part of her reason for signing up for yearbook was to prevent any more embarrassing photos this year, although she would never admit that to anyone.

Fred plopped down on top of the desk next to her. Reaching for the camera hanging around his neck, he pointed it at Christy and said, "Nice big smile for your ol' pal Freddy."

Christy did not smile. Calmly she said, "I don't want you to take my picture, Fred. Not today, not tomorrow, not ever. Okay?"

Snap! The bright flash went off in Christy's face.

"I don't think you're listening to me, Fred. I said *no pictures.*"

Fred's face appeared from behind the camera. His front two teeth were crooked, and his complexion wasn't the best. His hair clung to the top of his head like the skin on a pear. Katie had once said Fred was the kind of guy who should be arrested for using hair spray without a license.

"I had a dream about you last night, Christy," Fred said. "You were a famous model on location in Greece, and I was your photographer. You do believe that dreams can come true, don't you?"

I can't believe this is happening!

"I've already asked Miss Wallace if she'd make you my assistant this year so we can spend lots of time together. We'll have to go out on lots of photo assignments. Like every weekend for football games." Fred smiled, and she noticed a piece of something orange left over from lunch wedged between his two crooked teeth.

"Fred, I have a boyfriend." Christy never would have guessed how relieved she felt to be able to say those words aloud.

"Not that slime Rick Doyle, I hope!"

"No. His name is Todd. Todd Spencer. He's in college, and I'm sure I'll be spending all my weekends with him. So you see, I won't be able to go on any photo shoots with you."

Fred's enthusiasm seemed only slightly dampened. "Not a problem. I'll be with you every weekday, and Schmoddy-Toddy will only have you on weekends. We'll see what happens by the end of the school year. As I always say, 'May the best man win!'"

CHAPTER SEVEN

She Brought Raisins

"Oh, that wasn't the worst of it," Christy said, leaning against the kitchen counter that evening while her mom washed off a head of lettuce. "He took at least five pictures of me while I was sitting there listening to the teacher, and then Miss Wallace said I was assigned to take pictures with him at the football game Friday night."

"So what did you tell Fred?" Mom asked, her round face looking soft and interested.

"I told him I had a boyfriend, and if he didn't leave me alone Todd was going to beat him up."

"You didn't!"

"No, of course I didn't tell him that. I did tell him I had a boyfriend, though, and that I worked Friday nights and Todd and I had plans for Saturday nights."

"And do you and Todd have plans?"

"Well, not yet. But I'm sure we will. You know Todd is sort of a last-minute, spontaneous kind of guy."

"Christy, this is not the time to get in the habit of stretching the truth," Mom said as she sliced up a cucumber and added it to the salad in the big wooden bowl.

Christy snitched a cucumber slice. "I know. You're right." Pointing to the tomato, she said, "Did you know that tomatoes are full of vitamin C and something-noids?"

"Is that what you learned in science today?"

"No, that's what I learned from Michael." Christy gave Mom a rundown on how they had met Michael at lunch. "Then after school, if you can believe this, I waited for Katie at the car for at least ten minutes. She finally shows up with Michael in his beat-up little sports car, and she says she's taking him to 31 Flavors to introduce him to all the vitamins in jamoca almond fudge ice cream."

Mom chuckled and shook her head. "This could be a very interesting situation for Katie. Does she seem to like this Michael as much as he seems to like her?"

"I'm afraid the rest of the world has ceased to exist when he's around. It's kind of scary, though, Mom. She doesn't know anything about this guy. He's different. Not in a bad way, just unique. And he seems really interested in her—black eyes and all. I don't know. It doesn't feel right to me."

"Well, now's not the time to abandon her. Keep up with her in this new relationship, and keep those channels of communication open."

"I will," Christy said. "Are we ready to eat? Where are Dad and David?"

"Dad is in the garage, and your brother should be out front riding his bike. Could you call them both in while I put dinner on the table?"

Christy stepped out onto the front porch of their small rental home and called for David. A moment later the red-haired eleven-year-old came pedaling fast up their tree-lined street with his bike aimed at his homemade wooden bike jump. Up went the front tire as David let out a hoot and sailed through the air a full five seconds before landing on the grass.

"David, time for dinner."

"Okay, after one more jump," David said, pushing up his glasses.

"Mom said to come now."

"All right, all right! You don't have to get bossy."

"I'm not bossy. You just never come to dinner on time. And don't forget to wash your hands and put away your bike."

In a squeaky voice, David mimicked, " 'Wash your hands! Put away your bike!' Bossy, bossy, bossy!"

"David!" came a deep voice from inside the garage. That was all Christy's dad ever had to say to get either of them to straighten up. In his firmest, strictest, growling voice, he would call out their names, and both Christy and David knew they had better straighten up right then.

"I'm coming," David answered, sheepishly wheeling his bike into the garage.

"Tell your mom we'll be right there," Dad called out to Christy.

He was a large man who had worked on a dairy farm nearly all his life. Moving to Southern California had been a big change for him, and Christy knew it had taken him quite a while to make the adjustment. Now that they had been in Escondido for several years and things were going well for him at the Hollandale Dairy, Christy thought he seemed a little more settled. They still didn't have a lot of money, and her dad still wore his overalls in public, which embarrassed Christy, but in a lot of ways she knew she was blessed to have the parents she did.

Christy had some of those same thoughts later that week in English class. Their assignment was to describe someone they knew well and to use all five senses in the description. Her dad was the first person who came to mind. Christy jotted down some descriptive words the way the teacher had instructed them to. She wrote about how her dad's hands felt big and rough and how he smelled like cows a lot of the time, but on Sunday mornings on the way to church he always smelled like a forest, green and mossy. Sometimes the car would still smell like that on Monday mornings when Christy drove to school.

Her dad chewed Dentyne gum, which Christy listed under the sense of taste since she had chewed many pieces along with him over the years and that strong cinnamon tang on her tongue always reminded her of her dad. His bushy eyebrows and thick brownish-red hair made him look like an elf inside a giant's body.

For the sense of hearing, Christy wrote about the way his deep laughter tumbled from his huge chest and how, whenever he laughed, it made Christy's mom smile.

The last line of her description read, "Even though he comes across kind of gruff, my dad has a teddy bear heart. I've never doubted that he loves me, although I don't think I'll ever fully understand how much."

Feeling pleased with her conclusion and glad she had it done before class was over, Christy handed in her paper and used the rest of the class time to finish some of her Spanish assignment. It was due Friday, and she wanted to take home as little homework as possible.

As soon as school was over she would have to go to work at the pet store. She worked all day on Saturdays and went to church Sundays. That didn't leave much time for Todd and left even less time for homework.

When the final bell rang, Christy hurried to her locker and saw Fred standing there waiting for her. "Hi, Miss Chris. What time shall I pick you up for the game?''

"Fred," Christy said, impatiently spinning through the combination on her lock, "I told you I work tonight. I can't go to the game, and I can't take yearbook pictures with you."

"Sure you can! After the game. We could meet at one of the pizza joints where all the football players hang out and catch them with their mouths full."

"I don't think so, Fred."

"Come on, Miss Chris. We're in this together. Besides, your camera is nicer than mine."

"Would you like to borrow my camera?" Christy pulled it from the corner of her locker and offered it to Fred. It had been a Christmas gift from her Uncle Bob. She knew it was a nice one, but she didn't know how nice until Fred had drooled over it the first time she had brought it into class.

"Are you sure?"

Christy hesitated. Maybe it wasn't a good idea to loan such an expensive gift to this guy. Still, it would keep him out of her hair for a while. "Yes, you can borrow it on one condition."

"Wow, thanks! Anything. What's the condition?"

"That you promise to stop taking pictures of me and not to take any more for the rest of the year."

Fred made a face. "I can't promise that."

Christy reached for the camera. "Promise me, Fred, or else you can't borrow the camera."

"I can't promise that," Fred said, sadly handing the camera back to Christy. He looked dejected.

"Oh, all right," Christy said, pushing the camera back into his arms. "You can borrow it, and you don't have to make any promises. Just don't break it or lose it or hurt it, okay?"

"Not a problem. I promise I'll take perfect care of it, Christy."

Fred flashed her a big smile. "You're the best, you know. Anyone ever tell you that?"

"Just take good care of it, okay?"

As Christy drove to work, she wondered if she would regret her decision to loan Fred her camera. She decided to ask Jon, her boss at the pet store, what he thought. He tended to be a pretty good judge of character, or in Fred's case, judge of *a* character.

It felt strange going to work without Katie. Ever since last Christmas when Katie had landed a job as one of Santa's elves, Katie and Christy had shared rides to work. Katie had stayed on with the mall photographer and worked pretty much the same hours as Christy. Now with Michael to drive her around, Katie didn't seem to have much use for a best friend anymore.

It bothered Christy more than she had admitted to anyone. Especially since Katie was beginning to change. Not in any huge, obvious ways, but Christy noticed little things, like the way Katie had started to wear funky sandals like Michael's and how yesterday at lunch she drank bottled water instead of a Coke.

Jon was on the phone when she arrived at the pet store, so Christy went right to work, checking on the fish in the large aquarium section in the back of the shop. The soothing sound of the bubbles in the tanks and the gentle motion of all the fish made this hideaway Christy's favorite spot to go when she arrived at work and tried to make the transition from school to pet shop.

"Christy," Jon called from the front, "could you come up to the cash register, please?"

Christy slid the cover over a tank of angel fish she was feeding and hurried to the front. She had a feeling it was going to be one of those nonstop nights.

What she didn't count on was becoming one of the customers. By the end of the evening, she had a new pet to take home.

Christy tried to quietly open the front door around 9:15 when she arrived at home. The screen door didn't cooperate, and a loud screech announced her arrival. The eyes of both her parents were instantly on her, focusing on the rather large animal cage she held gingerly in front of her.

"Guess what? I got a bonus. From Jon. See, he thought I should have a pet since I worked at a pet store and didn't own any animals. He gave me everything free. There's even a big bag of food out in the car."

"What is it?" Christy's mom asked, rising from the couch and coming closer to inspect their new houseguest.

"A rabbit. I had a hard time choosing. You see, there was this little girl who came into the store with her mom, and she said she would pick whatever kind of pet I had. Since I didn't have a pet, Jon told me to pick a pet, any pet, and he would give it to me. So Abbey and I both picked rabbits."

"And what are you going to name it?" Mom asked, still appearing calm.

"Hershey. Because he's so dark, like chocolate. I can keep him, can't I?"

Mom and Dad exchanged glances. When Dad gave Mom a slight nod, Christy knew Hershey had passed the test.

"Not in your room, though," Dad said. "Keep the critter in the garage until we can come up with a hutch for it in the back."

"Hi there, little Hershey," Mom said, peeking in the cage. "What a cutie. Good choice, Christy."

"I'm glad you think so," Christy said, letting out a sigh of relief. "I felt as though I had about five thousand pets to choose from. It was so hard to decide! I'm glad you guys like little Hershey."

"Your brother will be thrilled, you know."

"I know. I'm hoping I can talk him into pellet-patrol when I'm real busy." Christy noticed her Dad smirking at the unrealistic goal. She knew it was a fat chance, but she could always hope.

"Todd called earlier," Mom said. "He's coming down tomorrow for the day."

"But I have to work," Christy said with a groan. "What time is he coming?"

"Before noon probably. Do you get off at six as usual?"

"Yes. I wish I could get off earlier. Tell him to come see me at work."

"David talked to him about some kind of skateboard park he wanted Todd to take him to. Maybe they can stop by the mall afterwards."

"Nothing like sharing your boyfriend with your little brother," Christy muttered on her way to the garage with Hershey.

Deep down, she knew she shouldn't be jealous of David spending so much time with Todd. It seemed to be good for both of them, since Todd was an only child and David looked up to him as the big brother he had never had. Any girl would be thrilled to have a boyfriend who got along so well with her family. And Christy *was* glad. It was just that she wished she could spend more time with Todd.

Todd and David didn't show up at the pet store the next day until after five. David wore a huge smile as he told Christy all about the skateboard park and how Todd had taught him some new, totally cool tricks.

"He's a natural," Todd said confidently.

"Hang on a second," Christy said, leaving Todd and David in the dog food section and slipping behind the counter to wait on a customer.

"Are you ready?" she asked the woman, who held out a dog leash and collar.

"Yes," the woman replied, "unless you happen to have the latest copy of *Gun Dog* magazine.

"All our magazines usually come in the last week of the month. We probably still have some of September's issue, but October's won't be here until sometime next week."

"Fine. Just this, then."

Christy reached for the leash to find the price tag. She noticed the woman seemed to be paying particular attention to Christy's hands.

"That's a charming bracelet," the woman said, looking at Christy's "Forever" ID bracelet. "Very unique design. Did you buy it here at the mall?"

Christy was about to say, "No, my boyfriend gave it to me." Then she realized that, yes, she had bought it *back* from one of the jewelry stores at the mall after Rick had stolen it and traded it in for a silver bracelet engraved with his name. But that wasn't what the lady was asking.

"Actually," Christy said, lowering her voice, "it was a very special gift from my boyfriend." With her eyes she motioned over to Todd, who was too far away to hear their conversation.

The woman followed Christy's visual gesture and turned back toward Christy with her face lit up in approval. "You are a very lucky young lady!"

Christy could feel herself blushing. "Thank you. I think so, too."

After she had placed the leash and collar in a bag and handed it to the woman, Christy remembered a detail about the bracelet she hadn't thought about in a long time. Last year when she was making weekly payments at the jewelry store to get back her bracelet, Todd was still in Hawaii. Yet some guy had come into the jewelry store and paid off the remaining balance so Christy could have her bracelet back. It still remained a mystery as to who that guy was.

For a while she thought it had been her boss, Jon, but he had denied it more than once. She even thought it was Rick since she thought she saw him at the mall the day she got her bracelet. It might have been, but Rick didn't seem to fit the profile of a benefactor who could keep a secret, especially when his silver substitute bracelet and his ego were involved.

It also occurred to Christy, as she rang up the next customer's purchase on the register, that she had never told any of this to Todd. Did he even know that the bracelet had been off her wrist for weeks while he was gone? Should she tell him?

Christy thought about the bracelet mystery again after dinner while Todd and she drove to the movies in his old Volkswagen, Gus the Bus. She wasn't sure how to bring up the subject. Todd was still talking about skateboarding and his adventure with David that afternoon. A heart-to-heart talk about the ID bracelet, the symbol of their relationship, didn't seem to fit in at this particular moment.

She decided to wait until after the movie. Maybe if it would be a real mushy one it would help Todd get into a more serious mood.

"Looks like we have a choice," Todd said, scanning the list of movies at the ticket window. "It's great when they're not all 'R's.' Do you think they're getting the hint in Hollywood that people want something other than blood and guts?"

Long lines had formed, and Christy and Todd slipped into one, even though they hadn't decided what they were going to see yet.

"Could be," Christy said. "What sounds good to you?"

"That second one on the list starts in five minutes," Todd said. "I don't know much about it, but the rating is right. What do you think?"

"Sure. Sounds fine. I don't know anything about it either."

"Christy!" came a loud voice from across the parking lot.

Todd and Christy turned around and saw Katie and Michael jogging toward them, holding hands.

They're holding hands! Why are they holding hands? Katie and Michael are really together. Katie, do you know what you're doing? You met this guy five days ago, and here you are, obviously on a date, and you're holding hands!

"Can you believe this?" Katie said breathlessly as she joined them. Her face looked flushed but happy. She was wearing jeans and a T-shirt with a Save the Whales slogan on it. Christy noticed Katie's black eyes had greatly improved. And she wore a new necklace made from tiny, brightly colored beads. "Todd, this is Michael. Michael, this is Christy's boyfriend, Todd."

The two guys shook hands, and Todd said, "So how did you two meet?" Christy thought he looked a little surprised.

"At school," Katie said, giving Christy a startled look. "Didn't Christy tell you? It was a designed meeting."

Designed meeting? Katie, a week ago you would have said it was a 'God thing.' What's happened to you? What's this 'designed meeting' stuff?

By then Todd was up at the window, and Michael quickly pulled some money from his pocket and told Todd, "Two more of whatever you're buying."

Todd paid for the tickets, and the four of them entered the theater. Katie chattered on as they found four seats together near the front, right when the previews began to run.

"Just in time," Katie whispered to Christy. The two girls were wedged together, with the guys sitting on either side of them. "Isn't this the cheekiest thing?"

"Cheekiest?" Christy questioned.

"Oh, Michael says it all the time." Katie giggled. "Isn't he terrific? Don't you just love this? Do you realize you and I are finally doing what we always wanted to? We're finally on a double date together!"

Christy smiled warily in the darkened room. "Yeah, this is great!"

Michael put his arm around the back of Katie's chair, and she snuggled a little closer to him as the movie started. Christy slipped her right hand through Todd's arm, and he grasped her fingers and wove them around his.

Todd squeezed her hand as if to say "Relax!" She gave him a squeeze back and settled into her seat. Katie was right. This was what Christy had always dreamed of, going to the movies and holding hands with Todd, double-dating with Katie and . . . that's where the dream didn't seem to match up. Christy had never imagined anyone like Michael in Katie's life.

Now that he was here, she didn't feel settled about him. Why couldn't it be Doug or Glen? Or any other normal guy from church? Why did Katie have to get involved with this strange guy, who most likely wasn't even a Christian? What was going to happen?

"We brought our own snacks," Katie said, reaching for Michael's leather backpack and pulling something from it. "You want some?"

Come on, Christy, relax. Enjoy this time with your friends. Sit back, eat some M&M's and try to act as if everything is the way it should be.

"Sure," Christy whispered back. "What did you guys smuggle

in? M&M's? Snickers? Ding Dongs?" Christy tried to think of what other favorite junk food Katie might have brought with her.

"Raisins," Katie said, offering Christy a small box. "We brought raisins and unsalted sunflower seeds."

"Raisins?" Christy repeated. "You mean those chocolate covered raisins?"

"Nope. Just plain, ordinary, healthy raisins. Michael says they're full of iron and something else. They're good. Really! Here, have some." Katie plopped the little box in Christy's lap and tossed a handful of raisins into her own mouth.

She brought raisins. Katie is eating healthy raisins! Oh, Katie, this is worse than I thought. You're really serious about this guy, aren't you?

CHAPTER EIGHT

Mice on a Mission

"Do you have any bottled water?" Michael asked the waitress at Marie Callender's Pie Shop and Restaurant a few hours later when the foursome stopped in for an after-movie snack.

"Yes, we do. Would you like anything else?"

"No, thank you. Just water."

The waitress turned to Christy. "And for you?"

Christy felt a little embarrassed ordering pie after Michael ordered only water. "I'd like a piece of cherry pie, please."

"Would you like that with ice cream or whipped cream?" the waitress asked.

She thought ice cream sounded good but turned it down. "No, thanks."

"Would you care to have it heated?"

"No, thank you."

"Good choice," Michael said, leaning across the table and confiding in Christy. "It won't be until the next generation that we'll see the side effects of all this microwaving we've done to our food. Can't be good for humans, I think. Best to avoid it whenever possible."

"Right," Christy said with a slight smile.

"A small salad, please," Katie ordered. "No dressing."

After the raisins in the theater, nothing should have surprised Christy, but Katie ordering a salad did.

"Not the iceberg lettuce," Michael added to Katie's order. "It retains pesticides even after it's been washed."

"Would spinach be okay?" the waitress asked, looking a little annoyed at Michael, the "nature boy."

"Sure," Katie said. Then turning to Christy, she mumbled in a low voice, "I guess it wouldn't hurt to try spinach for the first time in my life. What do you think?"

Christy knew this was neither the time nor the place to tell Katie what she thought. Instead, she returned Katie's friendly smile and waited to see what recommendations Michael might have for Todd's order.

"Pumpkin pie with whipped cream and a glass of water."

"Is tap water okay, or would you prefer bottled water as well?"

"No, city water is fine. Hasn't killed me yet."

The waitress turned with a swish, and Christy felt certain she was miffed with them. Christy didn't like anyone to be upset with her. Not even a waitress.

"So tell me about Belfast," Todd said to Michael, who jumped right in and in his wonderful accent talked about the political unrest in his beloved city. He told of being in a grocery store as a child and leaving only minutes before a bomb exploded. The bomb sheared off the front half of the store, but Michael and his mother were unharmed.

Christy enjoyed listening to Michael speak with such passion about his homeland. She had to admit his accent was charming, and he spoke with beguiling animation. Katie looked so proud to be with him. He was nice-looking in his natural, earthy sort of way. His thick, dark hair fit well with his fair skin and green eyes.

Christy had to admit his personality and looks were intriguing. If only he would say he was a Christian, it would make everything perfect.

When the food arrived, Todd said, "Would you guys mind if I prayed before we eat?"

"Pray for a piece of pie?" Michael asked with a laugh.

"I like to give thanks to God whenever He provides me with something to eat."

Michael looked amused. "But the waitress provided it. The cook prepared it. It's the money from your own pocket that will pay for it. What has God done to provide your pumpkin pie?"

Now it was Todd's turn to look amused. "God made the pumpkin. I want to tell Him thanks." Bowing his head, Todd said in a jovial voice, "Thanks, Father, for making the pumpkin. Thanks, too, for making Michael. You did a good job on both of them. Amen."

Michael laughed aloud. "I don't suppose I've ever heard a prayer like that before. You sure God heard you?"

Todd nodded and gave Michael a confident smile. Just before the first forkful of pumpkin pie touched Todd's lips, he said with complete assurance, "Oh, yeah. He heard me all right. God hears."

Michael took a swig of his bottled water and, shaking his head, said, "Your friends are a bit daft, Katie. Anyone ever tell you that?"

"They're the best friends a person could ever hope for, Michael," Katie quickly retorted, moving the spinach around on her plate, apparently trying to work up the nerve to take her first bite. "You won't find better than these two anywhere."

"I found you," Michael said, facing Katie and looking deep

into her eyes. "It's the luck of the Irish I carry with me wherever I go."

Katie blushed. But she didn't turn away. Instead, she met Michael's gaze and locked into a silent, visual embrace with him.

Christy looked down at her cherry pie. It was awfully hard to act casual when Katie was falling in love right before her eyes. Had she acted like that when she had first met Todd? It seemed so long ago. She was so used to him now, so comfortable around him. She couldn't picture herself being entwined in such an intimate exchange with him in a public place. Still, it was amazing to see Katie so in love.

Tomorrow, Christy decided, *when Katie and I are working in the church's nursery, I'm going to lay it on the line with her. If this guy isn't a Christian, which he doesn't appear to be, then she needs to break up with him immediately before she gets too involved.*

But the next morning, Katie didn't show up for her commitment to work in the nursery. Christy had her hands full with fifteen weary and hungry three-year-olds.

"I just found out the teacher for the three-year-olds has gone home ill," the church nursery coordinator said, popping her head into Christy's room. "I have you and another high schooler scheduled. Do you need an additional helper?"

"Definitely!" Christy said, retrieving a truck from a little boy who was about to throw it at two girls quietly looking at books on the rug.

"Mine!" the boy wailed. He burst into tears and tried to retrieve the truck from Christy's raised hand.

"The other high schooler is my friend Katie. She hasn't shown up. I could use all the helpers you can send me!"

"I'll send three junior helpers in right away," the woman promised. "Here's the lesson book. If you don't mind, could you look it over? It looks like you'll need to teach the Bible story today. Snacks will be at the regular time, and I'll be right next door if you need anything."

A mixture of panic and anger washed over Christy. Katie was the one who was good with little kids. She could entertain them on a moment's notice. Katie would be great at doing the lesson, even if it was last minute. She was probably off with Michael somewhere and hadn't even bothered to let Christy know she wasn't coming. This was unfair!

Fortunately, the three middle-school helpers were right at home with toddlers. They busied the kids with crayons at the table while Christy peeked at the lesson book.

It seemed easy enough, a story about seasons and how God is in control of all the changes that take place in this world. Some verses appeared at the end of the lesson from Ecclesiastes about there being a time for everything. She thought she had heard a song about that before.

I'm so mad Katie isn't here! She probably knows the song. She could have sung it for the kids. She should be doing this, not me!

Christy stared out the window at the church parking lot while she thought about Katie's desertion. The leaves were changing color on one of the big shade trees; several floated down and landed on some of the car tops like giant yellow and orange confetti.

It was a memorable parking lot. Her dad had given Christy her first driving lesson there. Last summer they loaded the bus for church camp in the lot. It had been Katie's idea to go, but she had backed out at the last minute, leaving Christy alone as a camp counselor to a bunch of fifth-grade girls.

Then Christy flashed on another memory of that church parking lot. Two years ago she had given Rick Doyle a Christmas present out by his car, and he had unexpectedly kissed her. Come to think of it, the gift for Rick and going out to the parking lot with him had been Katie's idea, too.

Christy realized she had a memory for almost every season in that parking lot. Maybe she could make a memory for this little bunch of young hearts out in that same lot. They could go for a walk and each collect one of those autumn leaves. Then they would come in for story time. Christy would put all the leaves up on the board and talk about how it's God who makes the seasons change. It seemed simple enough.

"Okay, now everyone remember to hold onto the hand of your buddy. We're going to be very quiet." Christy placed her finger over her lips and motioned for the class to tiptoe behind her like little mice.

Except for a couple of creative youngsters who added some tiny mouse squeaks, they made it to the parking lot without incident. Christy led them to the tree at the side of the lot and said, "Now while you're still holding the hand of your buddy, everyone pick up one special leaf, and we'll take them back to class."

Two little boys near the fence spotted their "special leaves" in opposite directions and tried to retrieve them while still holding hands. They yanked hard on each other's arm. Before a major scuffle could break out, Christy stepped in and helped Tyler find his leaf while one of the junior helpers took Benjamin's hand and helped him find his.

"Okay, buddies, everyone holding hands? Show me your leaves in your other hand. Oh, those are all beautiful! You did a great job. Now we're going to be quiet little mice again and go back to our room."

The procession seemed much louder than on the way out. Christy had to stop them at the door and press her finger to her lips once more. "I want to see only quiet little mice tiptoeing down the hall. Which one of you is going to be my quietest little mouse?"

"Me!" they all said loudly.

Christy quickly pressed her finger to her lips again. "Shh! I don't want to hear any noise. Quiet little mice don't make any sounds at all."

With exaggerated tiptoe steps, Christy held her new buddy's hand and demonstrated how quietly she wanted them to walk. It was working. They held hands, still clasping their special leaves, and tiptoed to the classroom.

The nursery coordinator happened to be standing by their door and seemed delighted at what she saw. "I wondered why it was so quiet in here all of a sudden," the woman whispered to Christy. "It looks like you had a special adventure."

Christy nodded and led the sweet parade into the classroom. As the coordinator watched, Christy said, "Now all my little mice need to sit on the floor and carefully hold your leaf in your lap. These are special treasures! God made these leaves."

The children took their places and looked at their autumn leaves with reverent awe, awaiting their next instruction.

"I've never seen this class behave so well before," the coordinator whispered to Christy. "You're a miracle worker! I didn't know you had such a gift to work with children. You should become one of our regular teachers. I'll talk to you about it afterwards."

Christy felt warmed inside. She did kind of enjoy this, as long as the kids were cooperative. She didn't do well when they were fighting and screaming.

"Okay, my little mice, you're doing a good job! One of my helpers is going to come around and put a piece of tape on your

leaf with your name on it so you'll know which one to take home
with you after class. I'm going to put all the leaves up here on the
board, and then I have a very special story to tell you."

Christy couldn't believe how sweetly the little faces looked at
her. They followed instructions and waited expectantly for her
story.

After she had gathered the leaves and arranged them on the
board behind her, Christy sat on the teacher's stool and held up
her Bible for all the children to see. "Do you know what this is?"
she asked.

"The Bible!" they all yelled. A string of comments and pushing and tattling followed.

Okay, so I don't ask questions unless I want a riot to break out.

"That's right, the Bible. Now everyone listen. Quiet little
mice listen to the story without making a sound." Christy waited
a moment while her helpers calmed the children.

"The Bible tells us about God. The Bible says . . ." Christy
quickly opened to Ecclesiastes 3:1 and began to read, "There is
a time for everything, and a season for every activity under
heaven: a time to be born and a time to die, a time to plant and
a time to uproot."

Christy noticed the next verse said, "A time to kill and a time
to heal." She didn't think a bunch of three-year-olds would understand that, so she skipped down a few verses and read, "A time
to weep and a time to laugh, a time to mourn and a time to
dance." Then thinking she might lose their attention if she read
the entire passage, which went on for another four verses, Christy
quickly summarized, "You see, there's a time for everything."

*I wonder if the person who wrote this lesson thought about how short
the attention span of a three-year-old is?*

She spoke a few minutes to the now-wiggling bunch about

how God is in control of everything and how He knows when it's time for things to change.

"Right now it's time for the leaves to change color," Christy explained. "Everything happens according to God's plan."

Just then the helper from next door walked in with a tray of juice and crackers, and all concentration was lost. Still, Christy felt good about having taught her first lesson to preschoolers. Some eternal secrets were locked inside those yellow leaves, secrets about God's design and His proper time for everything.

Even if the kids hadn't learned much, Christy knew she had snatched a nugget of God's truth for herself and hidden it in her heart. This morning had been a time to try something new, a time to teach toddlers. To her surprise, she enjoyed it.

As the children filled in around the small tables, a few fights broke out in their eagerness to get their snacks. This was the part Christy wasn't good at, calming down the wild ones. She had seen Katie do it with ease and wished Katie were here now.

Then, remembering how the verses said there was a time for everything, Christy gritted her teeth as she pulled apart two squabbling toddlers.

Maybe there is 'a time to kill,' and that time is this afternoon, when I get my hands on Katie for abandoning me!

CHAPTER NINE

Harder and Richer

"Well, do you know when she'll be home?" Christy asked Katie's brother on the phone Sunday evening. She had tried all afternoon to reach Katie, but no one had answered the phone.

"I don't know," her brother said.

"If it's before ten, could you ask her to call me? Thanks."

Christy hung up the phone and was about to head for the kitchen to find something to eat when the phone rang.

"Hello?"

"Hey, how's it going?"

"Todd, hi. I wish you were here."

"Yeah? What's up?"

"Katie didn't show up at church today. I called her all afternoon, and she wasn't home. I just talked to her brother, and he doesn't know when she'll be back. She's out with Michael; I'm sure of it. This is *not* a good thing."

Christy could hear Todd chuckling on the other end of the line.

"What? You think this is funny? She's serious about this guy. What's so funny about that?"

"It's not funny, but you are," Todd said in his matter-of-fact way.

"So you think I'm funny?"

"You sound like a mother, not a best friend."

"Todd, I can't believe you're making fun of me and treating this relationship between Michael and Katie like it's nothing!" Christy said, letting her irritation show. "He's not a Christian; she's falling in love with him. It's obvious. She's going to get hurt, Todd, or worse. And excuse me, but I happen to care about what happens to my friends!"

"Then stick with her," Todd answered calmly.

"It's kind of hard to stick with her when she's out with him!"

There was only silence on the other end of the phone.

"What should I do, Todd? I am her best friend!" Christy didn't realize how loud her voice was until Mom poked her head around the corner and peered at Christy.

More silence on the other end.

"Todd, are you even interested in participating in this conversation? I feel as if it's awfully one-sided." Christy had lowered her voice, but she was aware the intensity of her tone had not diminished.

"I'm here, Christy."

"Well, I wish you'd tell me what to do about all this. It's not something to laugh about, and it's not something to ignore. Katie is headed for big trouble if we don't do something. Tell me what to do!"

Todd paused before saying, "I don't know what to tell you other than to keep with her. Keep loving her. Pray."

Now Christy felt really mad. Todd prayed all the time about everything, and Christy tried to, too. But right now her best friend was about to make the biggest mistake of her life! Todd's answer, obviously, was too simple.

"It's not that easy," Christy argued.

"Sure it is. You're the one who's making it so hard."

"I am not!" Christy's voice came out wobbly with emotion. "I can't believe you are being so insensitive, Todd Spencer. I don't want to talk to you anymore!" Before she knew what she was doing, Christy slammed down the receiver.

What have I done? I've never had an argument with Todd like that. I've never hung up on him. He must think I'm awful! I can't believe I did that.

Christy immediately dialed Todd's number, but the answering machine came on with his dad's voice saying, "We're not able to come to the phone right now, but if you'd like to leave a message, wait for the beep."

Christy waited for the beep and in halting words left her message. "I—I'm sorry, Todd. If you're there, please call me back. I'd like to talk to you about this some more. Thanks. Oh, it's Christy. Bye."

That has to be the dumbest message in the world. What if his dad listens to it? Is Todd there and not answering, or did he call from somewhere else?

Christy thought of how sometimes Todd would drive down to see her and not call until he was in town, only a few blocks from her house. He would call to see if it was a good time to come over. What if he were calling her from downtown? It was an hour and a half back to his house, so it was no small thing for Todd to come see her. She felt awful.

For the next hour Christy waited for the phone to ring. She tried watching TV, eating ice cream, and doing her nails. She went out in the garage and gave Hershey a carrot and stroked his soft fur for a while. She felt terrible.

At 9:15 the phone rang, and Christy sprang from the couch to answer it. It was the wrong number; the person didn't even speak English. Finally at ten Christy forced herself into bed, but she lay awake in the stillness for a long time, blaming herself for hanging up on Todd, and worrying about Katie. It was *not* a good night.

She tried to call Todd again at 7:45 the next morning, but she only got the answering machine again. She knew his dad left early for work and Todd had classes on Monday mornings, but she had hoped to catch him before he left. The thought of spending the day at school without having apologized to Todd depressed her. It almost diminished her concern for Katie. Until she saw Katie at lunchtime, that is.

Michael hadn't arrived at their lunch spot yet. Katie was sitting by herself under the tree, so Christy rushed to get to Katie before Michael showed up.

"Katie," Christy began breathlessly, "why weren't you at church yesterday? You left me with a whole bunch of rug rats all by myself. Where were you?"

"Michael and I went to the beach."

"All day? I called you all afternoon, and your brother didn't know where you were."

"I don't have to check in and out with him. And what's with you?"

Christy decided to get right to the point. "You've got to end this thing with Michael. You're going to get hurt; I just know it. He's not a Christian, is he?"

Katie looked incredulously at Christy. "I don't know. It's different in Northern Ireland than it is here. With the Protestants and Catholics there it's more of a political thing. Michael believes in God."

"Oh, great! He believes in God. That's terrific! Do you realize what you're doing, Katie? You're going back on every standard you ever set. Don't you remember in Sunday school class when you were 'Katie Christian' up on the chair and 'Peter Pagan' pulled you down? It's happening with Michael."

Katie laughed. "You crack me up, Christy! You should see your face right now." Katie imitated her with a wild, bug-eyed look, shaking her finger in Christy's face. Katie laughed again. "Relax, will you? I'm not doing anything wrong."

"You're dating a non-Christian. Don't you think that's wrong?"

Katie thought a minute and said, "When you went to Disneyland with Todd a couple of years ago, would you say that you were a Christian then?"

"Well, no, I wasn't a Christian yet, but that's different."

"How is that different? If Todd hadn't spent so much time with you, do you still think you would have become a Christian when you did?" Katie challenged.

"I, well, it's not the same, Katie. That was years ago. Todd and I weren't really dating, and I wasn't falling in love with him the way I see you falling in love with Michael."

"You're daft!" Katie said, boldly using Michael's word as if it were hers. "You and Todd were dating, and you did fall in love with him. Only he was the Christian and you weren't."

Just then Michael walked up. Christy turned on her heel, refusing to make eye contact with him. "I'll talk to you later, Katie."

"What's with her?" Christy heard Michael ask Katie.

As Christy marched away, she heard Katie say, "She must have had a fight with Todd."

Now Christy was really fuming. It was bad enough that she

had gotten nowhere with Katie, but to hear her crack about having a fight with Todd was even worse, especially since it was true.

Christy found an unoccupied corner of a picnic table and tried to convince herself she was hungry enough to eat her lunch.

"Hey, Miss Chris!" came an irritatingly familiar voice behind her. She was *not* in the mood to talk to Fred.

"I got some great shots at the game Friday. You should have been there. I love your camera. Are you going to be needing it the rest of this week? Because if you don't mind, I'd like to finish off this roll of film."

"Fine," Christy said without looking up.

"Thanks." Fred was about to walk away when he stopped. "Are you okay?"

"Sure. I'm fine."

"Then why are you sitting here all by yourself?"

"I need to get some homework done," Christy lied.

Fred sat down next to her. "You're lying, Christy. You don't have any books with you. You're a terrible liar, I hope you know. Boyfriend problems?"

Christy ignored him. She felt terrible.

"Problems at home?"

Christy unwrapped her sandwich and prepared to take a bite.

Fred wouldn't give up. He bent closer and in a low voice said, "You can confide in me, Christy. Your dad is beating you, isn't he?"

His question prompted her to crack a tiny smile since the thought of her dad beating her was so completely absurd. "No, Fred, my dad doesn't beat me," she answered.

"Mine does."

Christy looked up at Fred for the first time. He was serious.

"Your dad really beats you, Fred?"

"Well, he used to, before my mom divorced him. I haven't seen him since I was nine. I don't even know where he lives now. The only reason I said anything was because I used to sit by myself at lunch every day when I was a kid, especially after he had beaten me and I didn't want to hear another person ask how I got the black and blue marks."

Fred lifted Christy's right arm and checked both sides. "No welts. You must be telling the truth." He smiled as if trying to make light of the subject.

"Fred," Christy said softly, "I'm really sorry. I had no idea."

"It's not something you go around broadcasting, you know. Besides, he's long gone."

"But the memories take a little longer to go away, don't they?" Christy asked. She almost thought she saw Fred's eyes mist over.

"Yeah, well, life goes on. Nobody has it perfect, you know. I don't even know why I told you. It's not really something I'd like spread around, okay?"

Christy nodded.

Fred let out a sigh. "So you haven't told me what your problem is."

Christy had almost forgotten her problems with Katie, Michael, and Todd in the light of Fred's revelations. "Oh, it's nothing really. I'm glad you came by, though. I feel better. Thanks."

"There's the smile I was waiting for," Fred said. Before Christy could stop him, Fred lifted the camera and pointed it at her face for a close-up shot. "Big smile, Miss Chris!"

"Fred, don't take my picture." Christy put her hand in front of the lens and blocked the shot just as the camera clicked.

"Hey!" he protested. "That would've been a great shot. Why did you do that?"

"Because I've told you, I don't want you to take my picture."

"But it's part of our relationship. It's my way of documenting our year together."

"Fred, we don't have a 'relationship.' Our year together is based on us being in the same yearbook class. That's all."

"You can see things your way, I see things mine."

"Fred," Christy began, but she didn't know what else to say. She felt frustrated. He had opened himself up and told her about his dad, and that made her feel more tender toward him. However, Fred seemed to use her sympathy to assume their relationship was progressing.

She decided to try ignoring him. It had worked in junior high with guys like Fred. Maybe he would take the hint if she ate her sandwich and didn't talk to him.

Unfortunately, Fred seemed content to sit in silence. He dug into his own sack lunch. Every now and then he would look up and smile at people who happened to notice them, as if this were a planned lunch meeting and he and Christy were together by mutual choice.

"I need to go to my locker," Christy suddenly said, stuffing the unfinished half of her sandwich in her bag and getting up from the table.

"I'll go with you," Fred quickly offered.

"That's okay. I'm going to stop at the rest room, too. You can't come with me there."

"Then I'll see you in class in a few minutes."

Christy started to walk away when Fred said softly, "And thanks for having lunch with me. Nine years is a long time to eat lunch by yourself."

Christy kept walking but thought about how, apparently, things hadn't changed much for Fred over the years. Part of her felt sorry for him and wanted to make an effort to be nicer to him.

He wasn't that bad. He had a pretty nice personality. If only he weren't so annoying.

The more she thought about it, the more Christy realized Fred's appearance was his problem. However, she had enough of her own problems and began to plan how she would start calling Todd the minute she got home from school. She vowed she wouldn't go to bed that night until she had cleared things up with him.

She finally reached Todd at 9:45 that night. He seemed fine, completely unaffected by their tiff the night before.

"I'm really sorry, Todd. I can't believe I hung up on you."

"You were mad."

"I shouldn't have been."

"Why not?"

"Because I shouldn't have gotten so upset."

"You know what C. S. Lewis said?" Todd asked. "He said, 'Anger is the fluid that love bleeds when you cut it.' I just read that the other day. You love Katie, Michael is cutting into that relationship, you're bleeding anger. It's natural."

"So you think it's right for me to feel this way?" Christy asked.

"I didn't say it was right; I said it was natural. The right way is hardly ever the natural way. The right way is God's way, which is supernatural."

"How am I supposed to get from the natural to the supernatural?" Christy asked. As soon as she did, she had a feeling she knew what Todd was going to say.

"Pray."

"That's what I thought you'd say."

Todd let out a low chuckle. "It's hard, isn't it?"

"Yes, it is. I thought the longer I was a Christian, the easier it would become. It seems to only get harder."

"Harder and richer," Todd added. "I guess we shouldn't want it any other way. All true love relationships seem to become harder and richer the more they grow."

Christy wondered if Todd were referring to his relationship with God, with her, or both. She thought the harder-richer part certainly applied to both relationships in her life.

"Well, I still want to apologize for hanging up on you, Todd. And I still feel concerned about Katie. I'll try to pray about it more. If nothing else, I've learned I don't want to ever have to wait so long to apologize to you again. It was awful going a whole day without things feeling settled and right between us."

"Yeah, I didn't like the feeling much either. I was over at Doug's when I called you last night, and I have to admit that when you hung up on me I felt pretty weird about calling you back, especially with Doug right there. He told me to let it go. He even said it was probably good for our relationship to go through this. For a while I almost thought he seemed glad you were ticked off at me. He didn't happen to call you last night, did he?"

"No. I tried to call your house but only got your answering machine."

"You want to come up here this weekend?" Todd asked. "Can you stay at Bob and Marti's and go to church with me Sunday?"

"I have to work Friday night and Saturday. And I have one more week to volunteer at the church nursery. I wish I didn't have so many things going on. I'd really like to spend some time with you. More than just a quick Saturday night movie."

"I know what you mean. How about next weekend then, if you're done with nursery duty? Think Jon would let you off early on Saturday?"

"I'll work it out somehow, Todd. I need to spend more time

with you. It seems like there's so much going on, and we're so far apart."

"Next weekend," Todd said. "We'll get together then. I'll call you this weekend after you get off work."

Christy didn't even try to hide her disappointment when she replied, "You mean, you're not coming down this weekend? We could do something when I get off work Saturday or maybe Sunday afternoon."

"I'd better stick around here and get some studying done. This semester is taking off without me; I'm already behind. I'll call you, and we'll get together the next weekend."

Two horrible, long weeks! Christy thought. It was bad enough going twenty-four hours without feeling that things with Todd were settled. Now waiting two weeks to see him again seemed like an eternity.

It hadn't seemed so difficult in the past, before they were actually going together. Then it was a treat whenever he did show up. Now it seemed like it was mandatory that they be together whenever possible.

Christy determined she would get off work all of Saturday the following weekend, and she would have her homework done so nothing would interfere with their time together.

Everything seemed fine until the next evening when Christy ran the plans past her mom.

"That's Dad's birthday weekend. I thought we'd do something together as a family," Mom said. "Maybe go to the mountains for a picnic."

"Todd could come with us, couldn't he?"

"Well, I don't know, Christy. It's your dad's weekend. He should be the one to choose who comes with us."

That didn't concern Christy. Dad liked Todd. Although Todd

had been included on lots of outings with Bob and Marti, he hadn't done much with Christy's parents. Certainly now was the time to start.

"I think we'll just have a birthday cake here at home," Dad said later that evening. "I'm not much for gallivanting around the countryside."

"It's okay if I invite Todd over, isn't it?" Christy asked. She could immediately tell by the look on Dad's face that the thought of including Todd in their quiet family celebration had never crossed his mind.

"Maybe not, Christy," Mom said, also interpreting Dad's expression. "Let's just keep it the four of us, and you and Todd can spend some time together the following weekend."

Three weeks! Christy thought it seemed like a lifetime. How could she contentedly wait three weeks to spend time with her boyfriend? Something had to change.

The first thing she thought of was her job. She would change her hours so she could have Saturdays off. Maybe she could work one or two weeknights besides Fridays, especially since Todd was busy with classes and wouldn't be coming down on weeknights anyway. That way they would have all their Saturdays free to spend together.

That Friday when Christy arrived at work, she approached Jon with the request. He looked thoughtful. "Perhaps if I can get someone to cover the Saturday hours I can give you Saturdays off, but I don't have any open shifts on weeknights right now. If you want to give up your Saturday hours, it most likely will mean all you'll have for a while will be your five hours on Fridays. Is that going to be enough money to put gas in the car?"

Jon was right. Five hours on her minimum-wage salary was not much money compared to the expenses she had, especially with all the added expenses that came with her senior year.

"I don't know," Christy told Jon. "All I know is that I have too much going on and something has to give. I have no time for a social life."

Jon made a clicking noise. She had heard him use that sound to get the attention of the birds and guinea pigs when he was about to feed them. Now he seemed to be using it to comfort her. "Time is a funny thing, isn't it? There never seems to be enough of it when you have something to do, and when you have nothing to do, there's too much of it."

"You're right," Christy said, looking as forlorn as she felt.

"Don't worry about it. We'll work out something. You might as well make time to enjoy your only senior year in high school." Then with a wink and grin, he added, "Let's *hope* you only have one senior year in high school!"

What was it that Todd had said? Harder and richer. He might be right about the richer, but right now things just seemed harder.

CHAPTER TEN

Thirty Percent Off

As Christy drove home from work that Friday night, she knew she needed to get a few things in order in her life. First on the list was to make peace with Katie.

The next morning she called Katie to ask if she wanted to ride to work together and plan to have their lunch breaks together, the way they used to. When Christy called, Katie obviously wasn't up yet.

"What time is it?"

"A little after eight. Did I wake you?"

"Yeah, but that's okay. I didn't get home until almost two," Katie said with a huge yawn. "I'm really tired. But I'm glad you called. I was kind of wondering for a while there if you were going to ignore me forever."

"Why didn't you get home until two? Where were you?" The instant Christy said it, she realized she sounded like a nagging old hen and was defeating her plan to rebuild bridges.

Katie paused and then in an irritated voice said, "We were at a concert in San Diego."

"I didn't mean to sound like that," Christy said. Then trying hard to change her tone, she asked, "Did you and Michael have a good time?"

"Yes, we did. Michael and I always have a good time."

Christy tried to sound encouraging. "That's great, Katie."

"Do you really mean that?" Katie asked.

Christy knew she couldn't lie. How could she get around this? She paused and found she couldn't answer.

"That's okay," Katie said. "You don't have to answer that. I know how you feel about Michael. I don't want you to lie to me, ever. I won't lie to you, and you know that. I want you to be happy for me. I have never felt so wonderful in my whole life, Christy. I feel as if it's finally okay for me to just be me. Michael likes me. Can you believe that?"

"Of course I can. There's plenty to like. You're a treasure, Katie."

"Do you understand what I'm saying? Michael *likes* me, Christy. He's the first guy who has ever been really interested in me, and it's killing me that you won't be happy for me."

"I just wish he were a Christian," Christy said.

"Why does that make such a big difference to you? I'm not going to marry him! We're dating, that's all. He's very open to God and to spiritual things."

Christy paused and chose her words carefully. "But Katie, you and Michael are getting so close so fast, and I'm worried about you. He doesn't have the same standards you do."

"Yes, he does," Katie quickly defended. "You don't know him, Christy. You don't know what he's like. You're too self-righteous to even get to know him because he doesn't fit your little perfect Christian standard. Let me tell you something. Michael has been more of a gentleman to me than Rick Doyle ever was, and Rick was supposed to be some hotshot Christian. Rick kissed me, and it meant nothing to him. Another conquest. A game. When Michael kisses me, I can tell he means it from the bottom of his heart. Our relationship means as much to him as it does to me."

"He's kissed you?"

"Of course he's kissed me. You and Todd kiss. Why are you being so judgmental? I haven't done anything you haven't done. I'm not doing anything wrong!"

Christy could tell Katie was fully awake and on the defensive. It would be difficult for Christy to accomplish much bridge mending now. Instead she chose to redirect the conversation.

"Is there any way we can take our breaks together at one today and meet at the Food Park in the mall? I've really missed spending time with you, and I think if we're going to talk, we should do it in person."

"I can't today. I already have plans," Katie said, sounding as though she was calming down some.

"How about after work? We could get together then. Do you still get off at six?"

"Well, actually, I don't work at the photographer's any more."

"You don't? Since when? What happened?"

"I kind of got fired."

"Katie, when did this happen? Why didn't you tell me?"

"You haven't exactly been available for small talk this past week," Katie said.

"What happened?"

"My boss didn't like me taking so much time off, so he let me go. It's for the best. I wouldn't have had any time for a social life with all the hours I was scheduled to work."

Christy knew exactly what Katie meant, but still, being fired was a horrible thing. "Are you going to get another job?"

"I don't think so. At least not right away. It's not a big deal."

"Not a big deal? Katie," Christy scrambled for the right words, "you're changing. What's happening to you?"

"I'm finding myself," Katie answered confidently. "And the good part is, thanks to Michael, I really like what I'm finding."

It was silent for a moment.

Katie spoke softly. "You know, Christy, I think of all the changes you've been through since we've been friends, all the guys, all the difficult situations. During those times I tried to be there for you, and I tried to understand. It would really help if you could take a turn now and support me a little. If you could try to understand and be even a little bit happy for me, it would mean a lot."

"Katie, I do want to support you. I *have* supported you in a lot of stuff over the years. Maybe more than you even know. The problem is that I'm watching you fall in love with a guy who isn't a Christian, and there's no way I can feel good about that."

"Well," Katie said with a sigh, "I guess I misjudged you, and I misjudged our friendship. I thought you cared about me more than you cared about your pious little Christian rules. It's exactly like Michael said, religion and politics are about the same things. They're all a matter of taking sides and taking shots at those who aren't on your side."

"Katie . . . it's not like that."

"Yes, I think it is. I need to go, Christy; there's a call on the other line. Think about what I've said, and let's talk again when you're ready to be a little more open-minded."

Christy had a hard time at work acting as if nothing were wrong. Everything she had ever felt about friendships, dating, and Christianity had been shaken in that phone conversation. How could things have changed so much and so fast?

During the next week, Christy pursued Katie and continued

trying to wedge back into their friendship. Somehow Michael kept interpreting the wedge as something to divide Katie and him.

After four tense lunches under their tree that week, Christy decided it would be best to leave Michael and Katie alone on Friday and pick up again on Monday. She felt she was doing the right thing sticking by Katie in this way. Todd had encouraged her to do exactly that and had warned her about getting her feelings hurt.

"Remember what happens with love when you cut it?" Todd had said. "The fluid it sometimes bleeds is anger."

That seemed to be exactly what was coming from Katie and flowing all over Christy—anger in the form of cruel remarks and defensive arguments.

"So is it just on Fridays and Mondays, or what?" Christy heard Fred's voice behind her only minutes after she had taken a lonely seat at the picnic tables. "Sort of a random first-of-the-week, end-of-the-week ritual?"

"Excuse me?"

"The last time you sat here was on a Monday, remember? Not this week but last week. I'm trying to figure out if there's any kind of pattern here. Do you only eat by yourself on bad hair days, or what?" Fred sat down beside her and popped the top on his can of Dr. Pepper.

"No, I only eat by myself when I don't have anyone else to eat with." As she heard her own words, Christy realized how pathetic she sounded. The awful truth was that she had spent so much time with Katie over the last few years, she didn't have any other close friends at school. At least no one who invited her to make a run to Taco Bell at lunch time.

"Not a problem," Fred said confidently. "I happen to be available today, and I don't mind eating with you a bit."

"Thanks, Fred," Christy said, her sarcasm showing through. She hoped no one would see her with him. His constant attention was beginning to bug her. He seemed to always be at her side, not only in yearbook class but also here at lunch.

Christy ate her sandwich in silence, aware of Fred's noisy slurping from his soda can.

"You know, Fred, you would be a lot more, well . . . attractive if you didn't make such loud noises while you're eating and drinking."

"Good point," Fred said without seeming offended. "I hadn't realized I was doing that, but you're right, it is kind of uncouth."

Christy gave him a slight smile and continued eating her lunch.

"What else?" Fred asked.

"What do you mean?"

"What else would make me more attractive? I mean, I'm not stupid. I know I'm not the kind of guy a girl like you would be interested in, no matter how much I hope and dream that I could have a girlfriend like you someday."

"Fred—"

"Don't worry, I'm not trying to compete with your boyfriend like I said I was at the beginning of school. I've given it a lot of thought. I'm not your kind of guy, and I know that. What I guess I'm trying to ask is, how can I improve myself so that I could one day attract a girl like you?"

Christy felt awkward. "I'm not sure, Fred."

"Yes, you are. You know what girls like in a guy. Pretend you're my big sister. What would you tell me? I mean, I'm a senior, for pity's sake, and I've never been on a date, never even called a girl without her hanging up on me. Could you sort of give me a crash course in self-improvement?"

Christy wasn't sure how to respond. No one had ever asked her anything like this before. Still, Fred was sincere, and he really did have a lot of potential. She realized that since his dad left when he was nine, he probably didn't have any strong male role models.

"Well, you might want to try doing something different with your hair."

"Like a haircut?"

"Sure. Why don't you go to one of those places that advertises they style your hair for what looks best on you and ask them to do whatever they think would look good on you."

Fred's expression brightened. "That's a great idea! My mom's been cutting my hair ever since I was a kid. Maybe it's time for a change."

"Sure," Christy said enthusiastically, "let your mom have a little break. Ask them to show you how to style your hair while you're there. You know, you don't need a lot of hair spray or anything."

"I use my mom's gel."

"You might want to pick up some of your own hair care products, too. They might even have a line for men, which would be good, because you don't exactly need the same stuff on your hair that someone, say, with a perm would need."

"This is great, Christy! You don't know how much I appreciate this. Maybe you'd like to come with me. We could go today right after school. You can tell the stylist what you think looks good on me."

"I have to work right after school, Fred. But thanks for asking."

"At the pet store at the mall, right? Not a problem. I'll come in afterwards and show you the transformation."

"Don't you have to go to the football game and take pictures?"

"Not a problem. I'll ask one of the other people on the staff to go this week. I would certainly think the future of my image is more important than a few football photos. I've deprived myself too long. The time has come to take bold steps!"

In a way Christy wanted to laugh at Fred. He was acting so exuberant, yet all she had done was suggest he do something normal with his hair. She could tell it meant an awful lot to him, though. And she was kind of curious to see how it all turned out.

Even though she wouldn't admit it to Jon or anyone else that evening at work, Christy was glad when she saw Fred pop into the pet store. Only he looked exactly the same. No transformation of any kind had taken place.

"Take one last look at the old Fred," he said when he approached the counter where Christy stood behind the cash register. "In an hour I will return, and you won't even recognize me."

"Have fun!" Christy said cheerfully as Fred waved and left the store.

A little more than an hour later, Fred returned right when Christy was getting ready to go on her fifteen-minute break. She planned to run down to the yogurt shop. Jon said earlier that they had Bavarian chocolate raspberry, which was one of Christy's favorites. Fred, however, had other plans.

"Well, what do you think?" Fred turned around slowly, showing off his very stylish haircut. It was the first time Christy had ever seen him without a lot of goop on his hair. The color had changed from a greasy margarine shade of yellow to a light blond. Along with the new hairstyle, the transformation make him look nice.

"It looks great. Fred, I like it. How do you like it?"

"I feel like a different person! And I have you to thank for making the suggestion. Now I need your advice on a shirt. They're holding it for me. When do you take a break? I'd really like your opinion."

Christy hesitated but then agreed. "I have a few minutes right now, if you promise it won't take very long."

"Not a problem. It's two doors down, and they're holding it at the front register." Fred headed out the door and waited for Christy to join him.

Jon exchanged places with Christy at the register. She began to explain where she was going.

"I heard," Jon said. Then in a lower voice he added, "If they're on sale, talk him into a couple of new shirts. Looks like his wardrobe could use a boost."

Christy hurried to join Fred. For the next fifteen minutes he directed her through the contemporary clothing store, pointing out an entire wardrobe of shirts, sweaters, pants, and even socks, asking Christy's opinion on everything.

"I really need to get back," Christy said. "I'm sure you can make these decisions on your own, Fred."

"Not a problem," Fred said. "I'm pretty sure I remember all the ones you liked best. You've helped me more than you'll ever know. Thanks, Christy."

"You're welcome, Fred. Oh, and if any of them are on sale, maybe you should get two. That's some advice a friend gave me."

"Good advice. I'll be back over to show you my final choices. Thanks again!"

Christy could have anticipated Jon's teasing reaction when she returned to her station behind the counter. "Perhaps you should consider fashion consulting," Jon said without looking up from the register where he was ringing up a subtotal. "Might pay more than pet store wages."

"All right, get all your jokes out now," Christy said. "I was only trying to be helpful. The guy asked me for my opinion."

"Let's face it, Christy. If you've discovered a natural flair for fashion consulting, perhaps we should consider opening a booth here for poodle owners. We'll supply you with swatches of colored yarn, and you can advise which color of puppy sweaters would look best on their little poodles."

Christy knew this was particularly funny to Jon because, even though he loved all kinds of animals, his respect for poodles had slipped through a crack. Jon thought all poodles were a freak of nature and not worthy to even be called dogs, let alone members in good standing in the animal kingdom.

"You know, it might help promote some business, Jon," Christy said. "It would be especially delightful for me to see long lines of customers in our store with each of them holding a poodle. Lots and lots of poodles. Yes, that's what this store needs. We could put a sign in the window: 'We Cater to Poodles.' "

A sly grin stretched across Jon's lips. "I'm going on a break. I'll be back in a few minutes."

Christy hoped Fred would pop in and out during the time Jon was gone, but Fred didn't show up. Jon still had his little grin on his face when he returned, and his hands were behind his back.

Trying to sound stern, Jon said, "Now I want you to take this, go in the back, and get busy marking all those jars of fish food. Don't come back up front until it's done." Then he produced from behind his back a large plastic cup from the yogurt shop bulging with a mountain of her favorite, Bavarian chocolate raspberry.

"Oh, if I must," Christy said with a sigh, accepting Jon's

thoughtful gift. "You really are too hard on me, you know. You keep treating me like this," Christy held up the yogurt for emphasis, "and I'll think you might be afraid that I'll quit on you one day."

"That's exactly what I'm afraid of," Jon said. Then snapping back to his teasing, he ordered, "Now get to work!"

Christy had just spooned the first mouthful of yogurt onto her tongue when she heard Jon say, "Sure, you can go see her. She's in the back."

A moment later, Fred—the new, improved Fred—stepped into the back room, decked out in a stylish outfit. Christy quickly swallowed the yogurt, nearly choking on it, and said, "Fred, you look great!"

"You like it? This was the blue shirt you liked. I bought it in green, too."

Fred truly had gone through a transformation. Now, standing before her was a nice-looking, stylish guy. She knew this was a breakthrough for him, and in a way she felt pleased with herself for helping in the metamorphosis.

"I owe it all to you, Christy," Fred said enthusiastically.

Just then Christy heard Jon say, "Go on back. Christy is receiving all her guests in the back parlor this evening."

Before she could turn her head, Fred, in his exuberance, threw his arms around her and said, "You'll never know how much you mean to me, Christy!"

Startled by the hug, Christy pulled away and turned to see Doug standing behind her with Jon right behind him.

"Hi," Christy said, turning to greet Doug. She could feel her cheeks burning. "What are you doing here?"

"Uh-oh," Fred said, taking a step backwards. "Is that brick wall your boyfriend?"

"Only in my dreams," Doug said.

"Oh, you too," Fred said, relaxing his posture and extending his arm to offer Doug a handshake. "I'm Fred."

"Doug," Doug said, returning the handshake. "I should mention, in all fairness, though, that Christy's boyfriend is my best friend. He's the brick wall you should be worried about."

Christy couldn't believe all this was happening. Did Doug think something was going on between her and Fred? He wouldn't say anything to Todd, would he?

"Fred is on the school yearbook staff with me," Christy said, hoping Doug would forget he ever saw Fred hugging her. "He was here doing some shopping and stopped by to see me."

Fred beamed a crooked-tooth smile at Doug. "She's transformed me into a new person!"

At that moment, Christy had to admit Fred's transformation didn't seem too evident. He still had the same personality and the same way of grinning so close to your face that it made you want to turn away.

"New hairstyle, new clothes." Fred stretched out his arms for them to get a full view. A price tag still hung from the inside of the right sleeve. "I'm a brand-new me."

"Looks like you're still thirty percent off, buddy," Christy heard Jon say. She wasn't sure if Jon was referring to the price tag or making a subtle hint to Fred that he still was a little bit off.

Picking up a box knife, Jon sliced through the plastic line on the price tag and handed it to Fred. "You know, this price tag reminds me of something. Now what was it? Does it happen to remind you of anything, Christy?"

"As a matter of fact, it does. The fish food. I'll get right at it, Jon."

Jon smiled at the guys and said, "Fish food. I know it's a rather demeaning task for our oh-so-popular fashion consultant. But the truth of the matter is I pay her to do this sort of thing."

Jon made his remark in a light voice, which made Christy feel relieved. Still, she knew that even though he was easygoing, he could get upset when there was a lot of work to do or if he was short of staff. She also knew it hadn't helped that she had asked to have next Saturday off. Jon had given it to her even though he hadn't hired anyone to take her place.

"Not a problem," Fred said. "I need to get going anyway. I saw a sale sign in the window at the Foot Locker. I'd better buy a pair of shoes now before I add up how much money I've spent. I might end up looking for a job labeling fish food, too, to pay for my new image!"

Christy and Jon exchanged glances. The thought flashed across Christy's mind that if Jon hired Fred it wouldn't be a problem for her to get Saturdays off permanently. Jon's look clearly said, "Don't even think about it!"

Picking up the sheet of already-marked price stickers, Christy began to affix them to the little round containers of fish food. Jon returned to the front, Fred bustled out with his packages, but Doug remained.

"Want some help?"

"Sure, thanks, Doug. You want some of my frozen yogurt?" She knew that was a pointless question. Doug loved to eat anytime, anywhere, any kind of food. Of course he would like some of her yogurt.

Good thing I took a spoonful when I did!

Christy was about to ask Doug what he was doing there when a voice with a familiar accent called through the doorway, "Excuse me, but is your name Doug?"

Christy recognized Michael right away and then realized that

Michael and Doug had never met. Why would Michael be looking for Doug?

"Yes, I'm Doug."

"And is it true that you were houseboating on Lake Shasta over Labor Day weekend?" Michael looked serious.

"Yes." Doug glanced at Christy for some explanation as to why this stranger would know they had gone houseboating.

Before Christy could let Doug know who Michael was, Michael continued with his volume escalating. "Are you the one who went Wave Riding with my little sister, Natalie?"

"Well, I . . . yes, I did go Wave Riding with Natalie, but . . ."

"Then put up your fists, man. I've come to defend my sister's honor." Michael played the part of an enraged Irishman in such a convincing manner that for a moment Christy forgot this must all be a joke.

Then she caught a glimpse of Katie hiding behind a bird cage, with her hand over her mouth. Katie seemed to be enjoying this immensely. Christy knew then that this was Katie's sweet revenge on Doug for the bop on the nose.

Doug had lifted his clenched fists to defend himself from the advancing, fiery-faced Michael. "Honest, man, I didn't do anything! Natalie and I went Jet Skiing. That's all! I'm telling you the truth!"

"That's not the story I heard from Natalie. She was a sweet, innocent wee lass until she met the likes of you! Men like you need to be taught a lesson, and I'm just the one to do it."

Michael's fists were up, and he was in a boxing stance. With a swing of his right arm, slicing the air between them, Michael showed Doug he meant business.

Doug looked flabbergasted. "I'm telling you, nothing happened!" Beads of sweat were forming on his forehead.

Christy wanted to break up the whole scene before it went too far. Her idea of a joke and Katie's idea were quite different.

"Wait," Christy said, stepping forward, prepared to explain everything to Doug.

Just then Michael took another staged swing at Doug. Doug, in an involuntary reaction to Michael's swing, lifted his right forearm to block the blow. Instead, he connected with Christy's jaw and knocked her to the floor.

CHAPTER ELEVEN

Truce or Consequences

"Christy, are you all right?" Doug dropped to her side and gently touched her jaw.

"Oww," was all she could say. It was more of a groan than a word, since her mouth felt too numb to form any accurate sounds. Her eyelids felt as if they weighed a hundred pounds each. Although she could hear everything going on around her, no matter how hard she tried, she couldn't open her eyes.

"She's unconscious!" Katie squealed. "Doug, what did you do?"

"Katie!" Doug shouted. "Where did you come from?"

"She's with me," Michael said. "We saw you coming into the pet store, and we thought we'd have a bit of a go-round with you. Didn't count on this. Can you hear my voice, Christy? Can you open your eyes?"

She could hear Michael as clear as could be, but her eyelids refused to cooperate. "Ohh," was the only sound she could form with her mouth.

"What happened?" Now it was Jon's voice. She knew he would be ticked off with all the goofing around. She wouldn't blame him if he became so upset he fired her. She felt certain this whole thing was her fault. The thought made her cry. Tears slid from under her closed eyelids, and Christy had no power to stop them.

"Look, she's crying!" Katie sounded panicked. "You guys, we'd better call 911!"

"Christy," Doug and Jon called her name at the same time. She could feel a strong hand lifting her head and someone else dabbing a tissue at the tears chasing down her cheeks. Then, as if the lock on her eyelids had been released, she was able to slowly open her eyes.

Blinking a few times and trying to steady her voice, she said, "I'm fine. Really. I'm okay." It came out garbled because of her throbbing jaw.

"I'm so sorry, Christy," Doug said softly, his face only a few inches from hers. "Let me help you up."

Doug took one arm, and Jon held the other. Christy rose to her feet and, feeling embarrassed by all the attention, said, "I'm okay, you guys. Really. I'm fine."

"Then how come you sound like a truck driver?" Katie said.

Christy tried to smile. "Ouch."

"You know, Doug," Katie started in, "it's not a surprise you don't have a girlfriend with the winning way you keep leaving your mark on any girl who comes too close to you."

Michael laughed along with Katie. "I'm Michael," he said, "Katie's boyfriend. I suppose I should actually thank you for giving her the black eyes. That's the first thing I noticed about her. If it weren't for the eyes, we might not have started a conversation."

Doug seemed more interested in Christy at the moment than in Katie's boyfriend or the cheap shot she Katie had taken at him. "You'd better sit down, Christy." Doug held her arm and directed her to a folding chair at the table. "I guess we'd better find some ice for that. Here," Doug said, handing her the plastic cup, which was now half full of melting yogurt. "Hold this on your cheek until I can find some ice."

"I already have it," Jon said, returning with an ice pack. "Put this paper towel between you and the ice. Otherwise it will be too cold."

Christy gingerly held the cold pack against her sore jaw. It was a doozy, and she knew she would be feeling it for quite some time to come.

"Can we call a truce?" Doug asked Katie once Christy had the ice firmly in place. "I have to tell you, Michael was very convincing. I'd say you've won, Katie. I don't think I could top that, and I don't think I'd want to try. Besides, it isn't fun when someone keeps getting hurt, especially the innocent bystanders." Doug gave Christy a sympathetic look.

"Sure, we can call a truce," Katie said, offering her hand to shake on it with Doug. With a hint of glee in her voice, she added, "But you have to admit that was a good one! Michael, you were award-winning in your performance of a big brother defending the honor of his baby sister!" Katie offered Michael a high five, and he cheerfully slapped his hand against hers.

"Had you going, didn't we?" Michael said to Doug.

Doug nodded and tried hard to push a grin onto his face.

"The funniest part, I think," Katie said, "was accusing Doug of being involved with a young girl when the truth is, he's never even kissed a girl before."

The room became silent except for Katie's laughter. Christy could feel all eyes on Doug. She knew he must be terribly embarrassed in front of Michael and Jon. Doug had made a vow that the first girl he ever kissed would be his wife, at the altar on their wedding day. Christy saw it as a noble, honorable goal. She especially admired that he had kept to that standard, and as a guy over twenty, he had never kissed a girl. The way Katie blurted it out made Doug sound like some kind of freak with a serious disorder.

"I think we should call a truce all around," Christy said, working hard to form the sloppy words that seemed to stumble off her lower lip. "Enough people have been hurt."

Katie sobered, and everyone focused back on Christy.

"We actually stopped by to see if you wanted to go out after work," Katie said. "Doesn't look like you'll be up for it now."

Christy shook her head. "But thanks for stopping." She sounded as if she had a mouthful of marbles.

"Are you doing anything, Doug? You want to do something with us?" Michael invited.

"I need to get going. This was supposed to be a quick stop to say hi to Christy. Maybe another time."

"We'll get going, then," Katie said, "before we cause any more damage. Bye, you guys. We'll see you later, hopefully under less bizarre conditions."

Jon joined Katie and Michael in the exit, saying, "Take it easy, Christy. If you want to cut out early, that's fine. I am counting on you to work tomorrow."

"I'll be here," Christy promised.

"Why don't you go on home?" Doug suggested. "You need to take some aspirin and get to bed. That jaw is going to hurt more in the morning."

"I'll go after I finish marking this fish food."

"I can do it for you," Doug said. "I'm sure Jon won't mind. Do you feel strong enough to drive home by yourself? I could follow you if you want."

"No, I'm sure I'll be fine. It's not very far, and I feel okay, really. A little sore, maybe."

"As long as you're sure you'll be okay."

"I'm sure. Thanks, Doug."

"Yeah, right. Thanks a lot for almost breaking your jaw, you mean."

Christy stood up and placed a comforting hand on Doug's arm. "It wasn't your fault. Please don't blame yourself, okay?"

Doug looked down at his feet and then almost shyly into Christy's eyes. "I feel really bad about this, Christy."

"Please don't. I don't blame you a bit. Don't feel bad about it."

Doug's grin returned. "Thanks, Christy. You're a sweetheart." Then carefully, tenderly, he slipped his arm around her shoulders and gave her a gentle side hug.

"What is this, the Annual Hug Christy Miller Fest and we forgot to put up signs in the window?" Jon said, sticking his head in the back room. "Hey, I checked with Beverly, and she can stay the rest of the night. Why don't you go on home?"

"Okay, thanks, Jon," Christy said, grabbing her purse and heading for the back door. "I'll try to be here a little early tomorrow."

"Mind if I finish labeling these for Christy?" Doug asked.

"Do I mind? Not a bit!"

Just as the door was closing behind her, Christy heard Jon say to Doug, "You wouldn't happen to be looking for a Saturday job, would you?"

Christy knew it was out of the question since Doug didn't even live in the area. He must have been passing through on his way home from college for the weekend. She never did ask him why he had stopped by.

Doug might talk to Todd before Christy did. She wondered how this whole escapade would be interpreted to Todd.

"Doug still feels real bad," Todd told Christy the next night on the phone. "He keeps blaming himself."

"I told him not to. It wasn't his fault," Christy said, propping her bare feet up on a kitchen chair and leaning back against the wall.

"I'll tell him again tomorrow."

"I wish I were there and could go to church with you tomorrow."

"You'll be here next weekend," Todd said.

"I know, but it seems like forever," Christy said with a sigh.

"Your dad's birthday is tomorrow, isn't it?"

"Yes. We're going to have his birthday lunch after church. Bob and Marti were supposed to come, but they're at a golf tournament in Palm Springs. He goes every year. It'll just be our family. I wish you were coming."

"What did you get your dad?"

"A flashlight. I know it sounds kind of lame for a birthday present, but that's what he wanted. It's a certain kind with an emergency flasher and a built-in radio. My mom said he'd like it. Doesn't seem real personal to me."

"Then why don't you make your card personal?" Todd suggested. "Didn't you tell me you wrote a description of him for your English class? Include that with your card. That's personal. He'll like it."

"You think so?"

"Sure. Dads like to hear they're doing something right every now and then."

Christy took Todd up on his idea and rewrote the essay on a piece of flowered stationery. This time she added at the end,

"Daddy, I love you, even though I don't think I'll ever be able to tell you how much." She signed it, "Forever, your daughter, Christina Juliet Miller."

When her dad opened his gifts the next afternoon, Christy started to feel a little flip-floppy in her stomach. *What if he doesn't like the letter? What if the part about him smelling like cows hurts his feelings? The ending is kind of sappy. What's he going to say?*

Her dad opened the card and read the page silently as she bit her lower lip and tried to ignore her mother's questioning glances. To her amazement, her dad didn't say a word. He folded up the paper, carefully placed it back in the card, and put the card back in the envelope.

"What did it say?" David wanted to know.

Dad didn't answer. He looked up at Christy, and she saw two teardrops start to race down his cheeks. She couldn't remember ever seeing her dad cry before.

"Did you like it?" It was barely a whisper emerging from Christy's still-sore jaw.

"Christina," he said, placing his big, rough hand under her chin and gently cupping her face. "You have given me the greatest reward a man can ever hope for in life. I'm so proud of you, baby."

Now Christy was crying, and her mom was crying, too. David kept looking at each of them, saying, "What? What's going on? Why is everybody crying?"

Christy had never expected this reaction. Todd had said all dads like to know they're doing something right, but this had turned into much more than a pat on the back for her dad. Somehow, Christy's dad had taken her feeble words and embraced them as a wonderful treasure.

It was a surprising and memorable experience, and Christy decided to write about it in her journal that night. She described the scene at lunch and her dad's reaction. Then she added, "It made me think about my heavenly Father. I don't often tell Him how I feel about Him. I know He loves me, even though I don't think I'll ever understand how much. And I love Him, even though I don't think I'll ever be able to fully tell Him how much."

Then Christy had an idea. If it touched her dad's heart so much for her to write out her feelings for him, how much more would it touch the heart of her heavenly Father if she tried to express her love for Him on paper?

For the next hour, Christy filled two pages of her journal with her heartfelt attempt at telling God how much she loved Him. In the same way that her dad's birthday lunch had turned into an emotional time between Christy and her dad, this hour of pouring out her heart to God on paper did something to Christy. She felt warmed and secure and closer to God than she had ever felt before. It was as if He were right there beside her, His heart listening to her heart, His eyes filling with tears the same way her dad's had.

Christy tried to explain it all to Todd later that week on the phone. He listened with understanding and simply said, "You know, if anger is the fluid love bleeds when you cut it, there must be something opposite that comes out of love when you nurture it. Some kind of sweet fragrance or something."

"Todd, do you realize how poetic that is?"

"Yeah, I guess it is. Are you surprised?"

"What?" Christy asked. "Surprised that deep down you're a romantic? No, not really. I've known all along that's how you think and feel, even though it doesn't come out very often."

"It's there, all right," Todd agreed. "I'm saving it."

There was a pause, and Christy wondered what he meant. Was he saving all his romantic expressions for her or for the future or

... (she didn't like the thought) ... saving them for someone else?

"There's a time for everything," Todd said. "A time to keep your innermost feelings to yourself and a time to share them. It hasn't yet been the right time for me to share a lot of my innermost feelings with you. But I'm sure you know they're there."

"And when will it be the right time?"

"I don't know. How do the leaves know when to change color? It's something supernatural that they do in a natural way when God puts all the right elements in place. Right now it's a time for us to . . ." He didn't seem to have the right word.

"To enjoy today?" Christy ventured, remembering her uncle's advice on the houseboat.

"I suppose. More than that, though. I'll have to think about that one."

Christy thought about it, too. She especially thought about Todd's words as she drove to school on Friday. A few of the trees along the way were changing into their autumn wardrobe and dancing about in the morning wind. She thought of Todd's question, "How do the leaves know when to change color?" and she thought about how there's a right time for everything.

And the time for me to finally see Todd is tonight! I can't wait to get off work and go up to Newport Beach with him. It's a good thing Bob and Marti are going to be home from their golf tournament today and they don't mind my staying with them for the weekend.

With a cheerful bounce in her step, Christy breezed through her morning classes and determined she would have a good time at lunch with Michael and Katie. The last few days had been pretty rough. It seemed whenever Katie tried to make a move to improve the friendship with Christy, Christy was in a critical mood. Whenever Christy tried to be patient and understanding,

Katie or Michael would say something that would set her off, and she would have to walk away before she said something she would regret later.

Today Christy wanted peace.

"Guess what we're doing this weekend?" Katie asked the minute Christy joined her under the tree. Michael wasn't there yet. "We're going to San Diego tonight, and tomorrow morning we're going out on a boat to go whale watching! Doesn't that sound like fun?"

"Where are you staying?"

"Remember that girl, Stephanie, we stayed with last spring when we went to the God-Lovers Bible study? Well, I got her number from Doug. She's still in the same apartment, and she invited Michael and me to stay with her. Isn't that great?"

"You're both going to stay at her apartment?" Christy asked.

"I suppose. She has two rooms, you know." The delight seemed to be draining from Katie's face. "I thought you'd be excited for me. Is that too much to ask? Why are you so critical?"

"It sounds a little strange, the two of you going off for the weekend and staying in the same apartment. Don't you think so, too?"

"I can't believe this, Christy. Why won't you take my word for it? Michael is a total gentleman. We're not doing anything wrong. His morals are as strong as mine."

Christy could tell that Katie was starting to get heated up. Her freckled face served as a clear thermometer of what was going on inside, and right now the red was creeping to the top of her head.

"You're really starting to get to me, Christy! Here I go and set this whole thing up with a bunch of Christians so that Michael can be around them and maybe even go to the God-Lovers group on Sunday night, and you make me feel guilty, like I'm doing something wrong!"

"I'm sorry," Christy said defensively.

"No, you're not. You've got your own set of standards, which I might add, seem to me to be a double standard, since you're going to spend the weekend with Todd."

"I'm staying at my aunt and uncle's. You know that."

"And I'm staying at Stephanie's. It's the same thing. You and Todd are going to be together the whole time. Why is it so wrong for me to try to introduce Michael to some Christians? Christians, I might add, who aren't as judgmental as you!"

Katie's words were piercing, and Christy felt her tear elevator quickly approaching the top floor, where all the wet drops would soon fill up her eyes.

"I need to go," Christy said, getting up and excusing herself when she saw Michael approaching. "I really do hope you have a good weekend, and I really do hope Michael becomes a Christian. I'm sorry I'm the way I am, Katie. I guess I just care about you too much, and I don't want you to get hurt."

Christy snatched up her uneaten lunch and was about to turn to go when Katie said, "I know that. Don't you remember what I said when we were on the raft? There are no guarantees. I know that. I know it's too late for any kind of a guarantee that I won't get hurt. The same thing applies to you and Todd, Christy. Or are you not willing to see that?"

Christy couldn't look at Katie. She couldn't talk to her when things got this tense between them. Trying to hold back the tears, Christy stepped away and greeted Michael with a fake "Hi! How you doing?" She kept on walking, heading for the lonely spot at the picnic table that had often been her refuge recently.

Today, of all days, Fred had taken her spot and was joined by two freshman girls, one on either side. He was wearing one of his new outfits, and as Christy approached, she overheard the girls asking how they could get their pictures in the yearbook.

"I'd say for freshmen your best bet is to do something out of the ordinary in cooking class. If you know when you're going to be baking a cake or something, you two can add some, say . . . green dye, and simply let me know ahead of time. I'll come to your class and record it on film."

He sounded so official. Christy had confused feelings. She didn't exactly want to join them, especially now that Fred had this new image that seemed to help him attract girls, even if they were freshmen. Still, the sad part was that now she had no one to eat lunch with.

At this moment, more than ever, she realized how few friends she had at school. Teri had graduated last year, and Brittany and Janelle, two girls she used to hang out with during her sophomore year, had both moved. Katie was the only person Christy had spent lunchtimes with for the last two and a half years. Except for Fred. Now even Fred had other friends.

"Miss Chris," Fred called out, spotting her as she tried to slide past him, "come here!"

Christy sighed, blinked back the renegade tears, pasted a smile on her face, and joined Fred and his fan club.

"What's wrong?" Fred immediately asked when he saw her.

I must be the worst faker in the world. I can't even hide my emotions from Fred.

"My jaw is still a little sore," Christy said. It was true. She involuntarily had been clenching her teeth while she was talking to Katie, and her jaw did hurt. "Makes it kind of hard to eat."

"Why don't you try some pudding or Jell-O from the food machines?"

Christy nodded her appreciation for the suggestion and noticed her camera sitting on the table. She thought it would be good to have it back so she could take it with her this weekend. "Are you done using my camera yet, Fred?"

"There are about four more shots on the roll."

"Mind if I take it back?" Christy picked up the camera and removed the lens cap so she could look through the viewfinder. "You didn't mess it up or anything, did you?"

"Of course not!" Fred looked shocked that Christy would ask such a question. She could see him clearly through the small box and had a sudden inspiration to snap his picture so he could see what it felt like. A sneaky idea came to her.

"Did you girls know that Fred sort of got a makeover last weekend?"

Fred looked pleased that Christy was still noticing and commenting on the vast improvements. She had him centered perfectly in the viewfinder. Now to get both the girls to move in just a little closer.

"Yeah, he got his hair cut, and he even got his ears pierced!"

Both girls cooperated beautifully by leaning in to get a closer look at the ear nearest them. They had expressions of curious amazement on their faces. Fred's mouth opened, and his eyes bulged at the exact instant that Christy snapped the photo.

"This will be perfect for the yearbook," Christy said.

The two freshmen looked at each other in delight. Their wish had been granted. Fred jumped up and tried to snatch the camera away from Christy. She held it over her head out of his reach and said, "Now, Fred. That's the only picture I have of you so far, and you have at least a dozen candid shots of me. Don't you think it's only fair that I get to keep this one?"

Fred plopped down hard on the bench. "Okay, okay. I get the

picture, Christy. Har-har. Just a little joke there. We can deal on this one. You give me that photo, and I'll give you back the ones I've taken of you."

"I don't think so, Fred. I think this picture will cancel out only the one from last year at the pizza place that Rick so easily persuaded you to take of me. That means I have about a dozen more of you to take before the year is over."

"That one last year was Rick's idea, not mine. Come on, Christy, have a heart!"

She was about to hold out to even the score when she remembered how things had turned out between Katie and Doug as the two of them had played their game of sweet revenge. As innocent as it had seemed in the beginning, someone kept getting hurt as their game progressed. Christy surrendered.

"Okay, Fred. Truce. I do need my camera back, though. When we get the roll developed, you can decide what you want to do with the picture."

Fred broke into a toothy smile. "Thanks, Miss Chris. You're the best."

Christy walked away with her uneaten lunch and her camera, deciding to shoot the last few pictures of the parking lot like Katie had suggested at the beginning of school. Something inside her felt right for having made peace. Maybe it was that fragrance Todd talked about, the fragrance that comes when you nurture love instead of cut into it.

Great! Christy heard a condemning voice inside her head. *I have this wonderful relationship I'm nurturing with* Fred *of all people, while nothing but anger keeps bleeding out between my best friend and me. It's time for a truce, Christy. How are you going to do it?*

CHAPTER TWELVE

A Handful of Regret

"Jon, I'm leaving," Christy called out to her boss at one minute after nine on Friday night as he began to lock up the pet store.

"Have a great weekend," Jon called back. "Say hi to Todd for me."

"I will. Thanks! And thanks for letting me have tomorrow off." Christy closed the door behind her and hurried to her car in the dimly lit parking lot.

Todd should be waiting for her at her home. She had her bags all packed so they could leave right away for the drive to Bob and Marti's.

She was so excited about seeing Todd that the keys trembled in her hand. On her first attempt to put the key in the lock, she dropped her ring of keys and bent to pick them up. Straightening, she tried the wobbly key again.

"Need some help?" a deep voice behind her asked.

Christy spun around and practically screamed. "Todd, I didn't see you!"

He opened his arms, and she wrapped her arms around his middle and pressed her cheek against his broad chest. She could hear his heart beating. Was it racing as fast as hers, or was it her imagination?

Todd held her for several minutes, pressing his cheek against her hair. "It's so good see you, Kilikina," he whispered.

Christy felt like crying, she was so happy and so excited to finally be with him, to feel his strong arms around her.

"I thought you'd be waiting at my house," Christy said as he let go and held her at arm's length, carefully examining her face. She wondered if he noticed the slight black and blue mark on her lower jaw, a fading souvenir of her collision with Doug's arm last week.

"I only got into town a few minutes ago. I knew you'd be getting off work, so I thought I'd come here and surprise you."

"You surprised me, all right! Where did you park Gus?"

"Over there," Todd said, motioning with a chin-up gesture over his shoulder. "Why don't I follow you?"

"Okay," Christy agreed, laughing at her trembling hand as she tried once more to get the key in the lock. "If I can ever get this door open."

"Allow me," Todd offered, sounding like her private knight in shining armor. He placed his hand over hers. It felt warm, strong, and confident. Together they unlocked the door.

"Thanks!" Christy beamed. "I'll see you at home."

Her hope had been that they could leave for Newport Beach right away. Todd seemed less eager to leave. He had brought a present for Christy's dad, which she had to admit was a very thoughtful gesture. It took a while before her dad opened it because Mom offered Todd some pumpkin bread she had just baked, and she kept asking him questions about school.

David, of course, had stayed up to see Todd and was trying to coax Todd into taking him skateboarding again.

"Okay, dude. How about if I come down next weekend on Saturday?" Todd suggested.

"Cool," David said. "Wait till you see all the new tricks I can do."

"Oh, yeah? Can you block a punch yet?" Todd playfully swung at David's right ear, and a wrestling match broke out between them on the living room floor. Mom quickly moved the coffee table out of the way and watched the two of them wrestle like brothers.

Nothing like sharing your boyfriend with the rest of your family!

It was after ten o'clock before Todd finally tossed Christy's weekend luggage into the back of Gus. Christy's mom and dad stood outside with them and gave the usual list of "to do's," ending with Mom's most important request that Christy call them as soon as she arrived at Bob and Marti's.

Christy climbed up onto the torn passenger seat of the Volkswagen bus. Todd used to have a beach towel over the seat to help keep the stuffing from coming out, but tonight it was missing. Christy had to find just the right position so she wouldn't get poked by the torn vinyl.

Soon Christy forgot about the uncomfortable seat and was busy chattering away. "I think my dad really liked that book you gave him. That was so thoughtful of you, Todd." She had to talk loudly because of the rumbling inside the van.

They talked back and forth nonstop for the first hour of the drive. Christy realized her throat hurt from talking so much and so loudly. She settled back a little and let Todd carry the conversation for a while. It felt so good just to be with him and to finally have their weekend together.

As soon as they arrived at Bob and Marti's, Todd headed for the refrigerator to pour himself a glass of orange juice. "You want some, Christy?" He obviously felt at home here since he was over all the time, even when Christy wasn't around.

"Definitely."

"Ice?"

"Yes, please. I'm going to call my mom and dad."

After letting them know the trip was uneventful and they had arrived safely, Christy was about to hang up when her mom said, "Have fun, dear. We sure find it comforting to know that we can let our seventeen-year-old daughter take off for the weekend and know that you're making good choices."

Christy hung up and thought of how different the warnings from her parents had been several years ago. It felt good to know that, despite all the up-and-down times, she had managed to earn their confidence. With their confidence came fewer restrictions and greater freedoms.

"I guess I'll get going," Todd said when Christy hung up. He placed his empty glass in the sink and said, "What do you want to do tomorrow, Christy?"

"Let's go out to breakfast," Christy suggested.

"Good idea," Marti interjected. She had entered the room a few minutes earlier. "I know just the place for the four of us."

Christy had meant that only she and Todd would go out to breakfast. How could she *un*invite her aunt? Maybe it didn't matter. What mattered was that she would be with Todd.

"Around eight?" Marti suggested.

"I'll be here at eight," Todd agreed and waved goodnight as he let himself out.

"He didn't kiss you good-bye," Marti said as Christy finished off her juice. "Why didn't he kiss you?"

"I don't know."

"Don't you two kiss?"

"Yes, sometimes."

"And what else?"

"Nothing else. Well, except hold hands and hug."

Marti looked to Bob and then back at Christy. "That certainly doesn't sound natural, dear. At this point I would have thought you two would be much farther along physically. I was planning to have a heart-to-heart talk about the physical dimension of your relationship, but you're not giving me much to discuss with you."

"I think things are right where they should be," Christy answered. "I have no regrets now, and I don't want to, ever."

"Very noble," Bob said. "Your aunt and I respect and support you two for your standards, don't we, Martha?"

Christy watched her aunt's expression change from critical to compassionate. Marti had Christy's best interests at heart, Christy knew, even if her methods were a little off sometimes.

"Yes, Christina, I have to agree. Your morals are quite commendable. Not at all the norm for most teens your age, I suppose. You are both intelligent people. I guess we can be glad that your school's sex education programs have been so successful."

Christy wanted to laugh. The open discussion she had experienced in her school had taught her about the complications and consequences of going too far, but she knew it was her relationship with the Lord that made her want to do the right thing.

"Actually, what makes the difference for Todd and me is that we're both Christians, and we're both trying to obey God."

"Oh."

"You know," Bob said, changing the subject, "I'd kind of like to sleep in tomorrow morning. Why don't you and Todd go out for breakfast, and the four of us can eat dinner together."

"That's fine with me," Christy said. "Is that okay with you, Aunt Marti?"

"Of course, dear. You two would most likely enjoy spending the time together alone. Knowing Todd's preference, it will probably be a casual sort of breakfast, anyway. We can make plans for something a little nicer for dinner."

Todd showed up a few minutes after eight the next morning. Marti was right—he had on his usual beach wear of shorts, sandals, and hooded sweatshirt. Mr. Casual himself.

Christy had ended up rising at six to shower, fix her hair, and dress. Even though she had on cutoff jeans and an oversized chambray work shirt with a white T-shirt underneath, she had spent as much time on her appearance as if she were going to the prom. Her makeup was light but precise. She had worked hard to get the mascara even on both eyes. Her hair, clean and combed, hung naturally without any of the clips or barrettes Marti urged her to use. Christy felt fresh and pretty, ready for whatever this day might hold.

"It's just you and me," Christy said softly when she answered the front door. "I'll explain on the way."

Todd led her out to Gus and opened the passenger door for her. Christy noticed the beach towel was back in place, covering the seat. Something deep inside her warmed, knowing that Todd had noticed and done something to make her seat more comfortable. She got in. Todd started the engine.

"Ah, Todd," she said, "by any chance, is this towel a little wet?"

"Oh, man. Sorry, Christy! I went surfing this morning and laid my towel there to dry. Here," he said, tugging it off the seat, "but the seat is still wet, right?"

"That's okay," Christy said.

"No, it's not. Hey, I know what we can do," Todd said, slipping the car gears into neutral. "You drive, and I'll sit on the wet seat."

"I don't know, Todd." The only other time Christy had been in the driver's seat and Todd in the passenger's seat was in Maui when he had been stung by a bee and she had to drive a Jeep on the precarious Hana road.

"You can do it! Compared to Hana, Newport will be a breeze." Todd hopped out and jogged around to her door, urging her to trade places before she had a chance to protest.

Christy slid into the driver's seat, buckled her seat belt, and popped Gus into gear, and down the street they chugged.

"I don't know where your aunt wanted to go for breakfast, but since I'm paying now, is Carl's Jr. okay?"

"Sure. Show me where to turn."

"Take a right at our intersection."

Christy looked at him out of the corner of her eye while slowly coaxing Gus down the street. She couldn't believe he had said "our intersection." It was the intersection where he had first kissed her and where he had given her the ID bracelet. She had thought of it as "their" intersection before, but she had never heard Todd refer to it that way.

A smile tickled the corner of her lips. She and Todd were really going together. Even Todd realized some of the things that had happened between them were sacred. Things like "their" intersection.

Christy turned right, and Gus rolled into the parking lot at the Carl's Jr. fast-food restaurant. She parked the van and turned off the engine, proud of herself for getting them there without incident.

"Looks like Gus recognizes an old friend when he sees one. He doesn't perform that well for just anyone, I hope you know,"

Todd said as they approached the cash register and placed their orders for two Sunrise Breakfasts.

The food was soon brought to their booth next to the window, and Todd reached over to hold Christy's hand while he prayed.

"So what was the deal with your aunt and uncle?" Todd asked.

Christy gave him a summary of what had happened after he left last night, including the part about Marti asking why he hadn't kissed her good-bye.

Todd looked thoughtful then, and leaning closer to Christy, he said in a low voice, "It's not that I don't want to kiss you anymore. You know that, don't you?"

Christy felt her cheeks blush. She hoped no one else in the restaurant had heard him.

"There's a time for everything," Todd said, still keeping his voice low. "It's kind of my agreement with God, to keep my life balanced by doing only what I'm supposed to do when He says it's time to do it. I'm not saying it's easy."

Christy sipped her orange juice and kept her eyes fixed on Todd. His silver-blue eyes were only inches away as he leaned closer and said, "There's something I've wanted to tell you, Christy. I hope you'll take this the right way. One of the things I really appreciate about you is that you don't come on to me. Do you know what I mean?"

"I'm not sure," Christy said, her eyes still locked onto his.

"You let me make the first moves, and that really helps."

Christy nodded, not exactly sure what he was saying, but agreeing that she did let him make the first moves.

"Girls have no idea what they do to a guy when they come on to him. Not only by touching him but also by what they wear. I love the way you dress. You always look good. Really good. Yet you don't try to show off or, you know, tease a guy."

Christy felt as if she were getting an education into the way guys think and, although she had heard some of this before, hearing it from Todd made it real and personal.

"I want you to know," Todd continued, "you've been helping make our relationship what it is by letting me be the initiator and by having so much . . . 'dignity' is the only word I can think of. You treat yourself like a gift. A treasure. And that comes across. It makes you so absolutely beautiful, Christy. You have no idea."

You're right. I have no idea what you're saying. I'm only being myself. I can't believe you're sitting here telling me I'm beautiful! This is a dream come true.

Christy felt the same way now with Todd as she had on the phone last night with her parents. Many times in the past she had wanted to run ahead of Todd and speed up their relationship. Now she was glad she had let everything develop at its own pace and in its right time. If she hadn't been patient, Todd might not be saying these things to her right now.

They ate for a few minutes in comfortable silence. It almost seemed to Christy that the air around them had turned fragrant. There was no mistaking a sweetness lingering in her heart after Todd's words.

"I have something else I've been wanting to ask you for a long time," Todd said as they returned to the van. "I keep going back and forth because I'm not sure it's my place to ask."

"You can ask me anything," Christy said, climbing up into the passenger seat.

"Is it still wet?"

Christy touched the seat before sitting down. The sun had baked that side of the vehicle while they ate. "No, it's dry enough. It's fine."

Todd started the engine and drove out of the driveway. "I thought we'd go over to Balboa Island. Is that okay with you?"

"Sure. What was it you wanted to ask me?"

"I guess I should just come out and say it."

"Yes, you should."

"Christy, I know it probably shouldn't bother me, but I've wanted to ask you about Rick. When you were dating, what actually went on between you two? I've tried not to let it bother me, but Rick said some things when we were rooming together last year that didn't sound like the Christy I know. I wanted to hear it from you. If you don't feel comfortable talking about it, I understand. I probably shouldn't even be asking."

"Of course you should. There's not much to tell. We went out a few times, I broke up with him. It wasn't the best of relationships. I got closer to God after we broke up. Why? What was Rick saying?"

Todd hesitated and then let out a heavy sigh. "Rick said you were easy. That you did whatever he wanted you to."

"That is a lie!" Christy said, raising her voice. "Rick said that about me? He is such a jerk! How could you believe him? Todd! I can't believe you thought—"

"Hey, relax. I didn't say I believed him. I know you. Like I said, it's been bothering me, so I wanted to talk with you about it."

"Todd," Christy began with a lower, calmer voice, "Rick is the kind of guy who seems to get whatever he wants. For some reason, he decided he wanted me. It's all a lot clearer to me now that I know what kind of guy he is, but at the time I have to admit I was a little misty-minded. I thought he really liked me just because I was me. He has a way with words. I know now that some guys can manipulate girls by what they say. At the time, I don't know, I guess I really wanted a boyfriend. I thought I needed one. You were leaving for Hawaii, and Rick was so nice to me. . . ."

"Hey, you don't have to apologize for anything, Christy. I'm not asking you to give me an account of your relationship with Rick. That's between God and you. I guess I needed to hear from you that he didn't take advantage of you."

"He tried more than once. We kissed a few times, but I always pulled away. I know it made him mad. It just didn't feel right to me."

"That's all, then? Some kissing?"

"And a few hugs," Christy said. "Nothing else. I can't believe he made it sound like more than that."

"I'm sure with some other girls it has been. Maybe it sort of bent his ego out of shape since it wasn't more than that with you," Todd said.

They had reached the ramp to the Balboa Island Ferry, and Gus's tires clanged loudly up the metal incline. Todd stopped the engine and suggested they climb out for the short ride across to Balboa Island.

Christy stood by the side, gazing out at the blue water in the bay. The October morning breeze chilled her, and she crossed her arms to keep warm. Todd came and stood behind her, wrapping his big arms around her and burying his nose in her hair.

A sudden flash of a memory came to her of a time when Rick had held her like this and whispered sweet words in her ear. Now it made her mad that she had ever gone out with Rick. If only she had waited, she could have shared all these boyfriend-girlfriend moments and feelings with just Todd.

"Hey," Todd said softly, "why are you all tensed up?"

"I'm mad. Mad that I ever went out with Rick. Mad at myself for not waiting for you. And before you say that this anger is bleeding out of love that's been cut, it's not! Love was not even a part of my relationship with Rick. Not real love."

"Christy, you're being too hard on yourself. Think back on when you were with Rick. There were some good times, too, weren't there? A few fragrant memories?"

Todd was right. There had been some special moments with Rick—on the swings at the park, flying kites at the beach, their first date at the fancy Villa Nova Restaurant.

"Yes, there were some good times. It wasn't all bad, and he didn't do anything to ruin my life forever."

"Here," Todd said, letting go of Christy and coming around to face her with his hands cupped together in front of her. "Put all your regrets in here."

"What?"

"In my hands. Put all those regrets and bad feelings in here. Sort out the good stuff and keep that part in your heart. Put the rest in here."

Christy gave Todd a wary look. Then playing along, she held her fingers over his hands and pretended to be sprinkling all the bad stuff into his open palms. "There. Now what are you going to do with my little pile of ashes?"

"Same thing God says He does with all our sins," Todd said, pretending to toss the handful of regrets into the wind and out to the ocean. "He separates them from us as far as the east is from the west, and He buries them in the deepest sea."

Then looking into Christy's eyes, Todd's silver-blues shot straight to her heart as he said confidently, "God doesn't hold this against you. I don't hold this against you. Why should you hold it against yourself? It's all gone, Christy. Choose to remember only the good parts, okay?"

Christy drew in a deep breath of the chill morning air. "Okay."

Todd smiled, and she could see the dimple in his right cheek. "God likes giving us beauty for our ashes when we let Him," he said.

The ferry motored into the harbor, and the two cars behind Gus started up their engines. "Time to go," Todd said as he opened the door for Christy to get in. They drove off the ferry and down the narrow street. On the second corner to the left, a fun-looking yard sale was in progress.

"Let's stop," Christy said. "Is there any place to park?"

"Looks pretty tight. Why don't you hop out, and I'll circle the block."

Christy did, and the first thing she saw was an old bookshelf. The sticker said five dollars. Before she had a chance to change her mind, Christy reached in her purse for a five-dollar bill and bought the bookshelf. Todd turned the corner, and she flagged him down, proudly pointing to her purchase. He double-parked Gus, popped open the back, and slid in the bookshelf. Then they jumped back in Gus and sputtered down the street.

"Isn't it cute! I needed something in my room for all my junk. This will be perfect. Of course, it needs some paint. You want to help me paint it?"

Todd had a wide grin across his face. "That had to be the fastest shopping spree on record! Sure, I'll help you. We can stop by the paint store and paint it today so it'll be dry enough to take home tomorrow."

"Perfect!' Christy said excitedly. "It's so cute. Don't you think it's cute?"

"If you say so," Todd said, the grin still flickering across his face.

CHAPTER THIRTEEN

To Cherish

"How's it going?" Todd asked when he stepped out to the front of Marti's house, where Christy had her bookshelf balanced on a carpet of newspapers. Uncle Bob had sanded it down for her with his electric sander, and now it was ready for the paint.

Christy had been stirring the paint while Todd was inside making sandwiches. He handed her a paper plate with a huge turkey sandwich and a mound of potato chips.

"You must think I'm going to work up a pretty big appetite," Christy said.

"I figured whatever you didn't eat I would," Todd said, chomping into his equally large sandwich. "Marti said she had made reservations somewhere for the four of us for dinner. That's several hours away, though."

"Well, I'm ready to start painting," Christy said. "If you want some of my sandwich, go ahead. Leave me about three bites, though."

"I can do this," Todd said, sitting on the steps and taking another bite of sandwich. "You work; I'll supervise."

Christy dipped the brush into the bucket of paint and started with the inside.

"Good thinking, doing the inside first," Todd praised. "Don't forget to do the undersides of the shelves, too."

"Todd, do you think white is the best color? I'm wondering if I should have done it in a soft yellow or maybe a real faint, dusty rose."

"White is good."

"No, really, don't you think we should have picked something a little more exciting? Maybe a pale, sky blue."

"White is good."

Christy turned to face Todd and waved the wet paint brush at him. "You don't really care, do you?"

"I think white is good." He bit into his sandwich. "Goes with everything, it's easy to, ah . . . match with anything. White is good."

Christy gave him a little smirk and went back to work. "I really like this bookshelf, I hope you know. It's going to be a new home for a lot of old mementos. Most of them from you."

"From me? All I ever gave you was a bracelet. Oh, and maybe that coconut I mailed you from Oahu."

"Keep thinking," Christy said. "Remember the flowers you gave me?"

"Oh, yeah. Those little white ones when you were leaving to go back to Wisconsin."

"Carnations, Todd. They were carnations. I dried them and saved them in a Folgers coffee can. It was all I could find to put them in when we moved out here to California. I still have them."

"Amazing," Todd said, stuffing in the last bite. "That had to be like three summers ago."

"Yep. The same summer we went to Disneyland, and you bought me the stuffed Winnie the Pooh. Remember?"

"Oh, yeah. Disneyland. I remember," Todd said, leaning back

in his chair and folding his arms across his chest. "I wanted to impress you so much, I let you think I was paying for everything. Then when I gave you back your aunt's money at the end of the night, I thought you were going to kill me!" Todd laughed. "Didn't you throw your shoes at me or something?"

Christy laughed. "Yes, can you believe it? Here I thought you were going to kiss me good night, and instead, you hand me this wad of money and tell me the only reason you took me was because my aunt talked you into it."

"You thought I was going to kiss you?" Todd looked surprised.

"Of course I did!"

"No way, man, I was too chicken! I'd never kissed a girl before. I have to admit, I thought about it all day, but when the moment came, there was no way."

"Do you remember the first time you did kiss me?" Christy asked.

"Of course. I'll never forget it," Todd said. "It was only two days later, but everything had changed. Tracy told me you'd given your heart to the Lord and that you were leaving to go back to Wisconsin. So when I caught up with you at our intersection, I remember thinking, 'Okay, Todd, it's now or never.' " He looked so content as he said it. "And it was 'now.' I'll never forget it."

"Me neither," Christy said. She painted a bit more on the inside and said, "So are you going to help me with the rest of this?"

"Sure. Hand me a brush. You want me to do the front or the back?"

"Whatever you want."

Todd squatted down right behind Christy and put his arm out next to hers. "How about if we do it side by side? I'll come along and clean up all your mistakes."

"Oh, getting a bit overly confident of ourselves, aren't we?"

Christy teased. "And what makes you so sure I'm going to make any boo-boos?"

"Just a precaution," Todd said.

She loved feeling him this close, with his broad shoulders hovering over her. Christy tilted her head back and leaned gently against his chest. "Now this is what I call teamwork," she said.

Just then Christy heard a familiar, but not so favorite, sound— a camera clicking. This time it was Bob, not Fred, who hid behind the lens.

"Thought I'd see how the camera was working," Bob said, his merry eyes twinkling. "Don't let me bother you two."

"Christy was just asking me how I thought she'd look with a bit of paint on her nose, and I was about to show her," Todd said, lifting his paint brush and playfully preparing to make his mark.

"Fine, fine," Bob said, positioning the camera closer. "Don't let me stop you."

"Wait!" Christy squealed as she heard the camera click. "The paint goes on the bookshelf, not me!"

"Oh, right. Now what exactly does a bookshelf look like? Oh, here's one." With that, Todd dabbed a bit of paint on the end of Christy's nose.

"That's not a bookshelf! This is," Christy said, and with that, she dotted Todd's right cheek. "Oh, that wasn't a bookshelf. That was a dimple. Now where did that bookshelf go?"

"I don't have any dimples," Todd said, touching his cheek.

"Oh, yes you do. I noticed it the first time we went to Balboa on the tandem bike. Remember? We bought Balboa Bars."

"That's right," Todd said. "And you got a streak of chocolate right there on your face." He outlined the memory with a stroke of the paint brush. "And it stayed on the rest of the day!"

"You asked for it, *dude!*" Christy teased. "This is for never writing to me *ever!*" She painted a stripe up his arm.

Click went the camera.

"Hey, I sent you a coconut!"

"And this is for all the times you've thrown me in the ocean!" Another stripe went up his other arm.

"Whoops!" Bob said. "That was the last shot. Guess you'll have to call a truce."

Christy and Todd looked at each other. They each had their paint brushes poised and ready to strike.

"Truce?" Christy suggested.

"Truce," Todd agreed, and as if they were slapping high fives, they whapped their paint brushes together and were instantly showered in a spray of tiny polka dots.

"Look at us!" Christy said, cracking up at the sight of Todd with paint in his face, hair, everywhere. "Do I look as funny as you?"

"No, funnier."

After they finished laughing and wiping the paint from their eyelashes, Todd and Christy set to work. Within an hour they had transformed the bookshelf into a white home for all of Christy's mementos.

Standing back to admire their work, Christy said, "I don't know. A dusty rose would have been nice."

"White is good," Todd assured her. "After it dries, you'll see."

Todd drove the few blocks to his house to shower and change while Christy went to clean up in the bathroom off her guest room. Little flecks of paint clung to her arms and to her eyebrows. It was a tedious process, getting herself back to normal, and she needed an extra dose of lotion when she was done. She changed into a pair of jeans and a white cotton shirt, rolling up the long sleeves.

Todd was already downstairs, watching TV with her uncle. "Did you check on it yet?" Christy asked.

"Check on what?"

"The bookshelf. I want to see if it's dry."

"It won't be dry until tomorrow," Bob said. "Did Marti tell you we're going out to dinner in about an hour? She's made reservations at a new place in Huntington Beach."

Todd rose from the couch and said, "Sounds like we have enough time for a walk on the beach."

Christy smiled at the good-looking, bronzed young man walking toward her. His short, sandy blond hair was still wet. His blue eyes met hers, and he held out his hand, inviting her to take a walk. She slipped her hand into his, and they walked together out the sliding door. Kicking off their shoes, they let their feet sink into the cool sand.

"It's going to be quite a sunset tonight," Todd said. "See how the clouds are sort of puffing up there on the horizon? Wait until the sun hits the ocean. They'll all turn pink and orange."

"The dust beneath His feet," Christy said.

"You remembered," Todd said, squeezing her hand. "Yeah, those clouds are going to turn into some major mounds of dust tonight. Looks like God has been busy walking around our side of the earth today."

They made their way through the sand, hand in hand, down to the firm, wet sand along the shoreline and walked together in silence. Todd's thumb automatically rubbed the chain on her Forever bracelet.

That reminded Christy she had never asked him if he knew who paid for her to get it back. "Todd, I want to ask you something. You had some stored up questions for me this morning; now I have one for you. I guess the first thing I should ask is, did you know Rick sort of stole my bracelet?"

Todd stopped walking and faced her. "What do you mean?"

Christy explained how she had taken off her bracelet, left it in her purse in Rick's car, and then thought it was lost. She later found out he had used it as a trade-in on a new bracelet—a clunky silver one that said "Rick." Christy figured out he had taken it, and after breaking up with him, she tried to buy it back from the jewelry store where he had hocked it.

"I didn't know any of this," Todd said, still standing in one spot as the tide rose and lapped up, burying their feet in the sand.

"My next question was if you had been the one who paid the balance so I could get it back. All the jeweler would say was that it was some guy."

"It wasn't me. I didn't even know. Do you think it was Rick?"

"I did for a while, but the more I think about it the more I doubt it."

"Your dad maybe? Bob?" Todd suggested.

"Maybe. Although I don't think either of them knew about the whole incident. I guess it'll remain a mystery."

Todd wiggled his feet out of the sand and started down the beach, holding even tighter to Christy's hand. "I don't mind it being a mystery as long as you have the bracelet back."

"I guess I can live with a little mystery, too," Christy said. "The whole thing only makes me madder at Rick."

"Wait a second. Wasn't that part of the regrets we tossed out to sea this morning?" Todd motioned out to the ocean. "You want to try swimming out there and gathering up all the ashes again? It's not worth it, Christy. Let it go."

"You're right," Christy agreed, nestling her head against Todd's shoulder. Then after a brief pause she added, "I wish I could let this whole thing with Katie and Michael just go, too."

"That's different," Todd said. "You can't let that go. You have to hold on tighter than ever."

"But when I tell her he's not a Christian and she should drop him, she turns on me. I hate causing all this conflict."

"So are you going to change your opinion on dating non-Christians?"

"No. I can't. I feel too strongly about it," Christy said.

"Then what can you change?"

Christy thought. She wasn't sure. When Todd said, "change," it reminded her of when he had said, "How do the leaves know when it's time to change?" His answer had been that it's something supernatural that God brings about in a natural way.

"I guess I can't change anything. Only God can. I can ask Him to do something supernatural in a natural way."

Todd squeezed her hand again. "And you can ask Him and ask Him and ask Him again. Really good answers come from persistent prayers."

"But in the meantime, everything is different between Katie and me."

"Yes," Todd agreed.

"It's impossible for me to change how I feel about her dating Michael."

"Yes."

"I wish it weren't so hard and that it didn't take so long for God to answer prayers."

"I agree."

"How can you take it so lightly?" Christy asked.

"I don't take it lightly. I've been praying for Katie and Michael ever since that night we met up with them at the movies. The only thing that gives me hope is that God said there is a time for everything. This is a time for Katie to make some major choices, and this is a time for you to stick close to her. Then, depending on how her choices go, you two will probably soon have either a time to mourn together or a time to dance. For me, it's a time to pray."

"Could we do that right now?" Christy asked.

Todd led her a few feet up to the drier sand, and the two of them sat close together, holding hands and praying for Katie and Michael. When they looked up, the sun had dipped its toes into the ocean. As Todd had predicted, the "dust of His feet" clouds were ablaze with California sunset colors—ambers, tangerines, lemons, and dusty rose.

Although Christy couldn't explain how, she felt everything with Katie was going to turn out okay. Maybe it was simply because Christy had finally released the situation to the Lord as she and Todd had prayed. Or maybe it was because of the incredible sunset. It made everything else seem small compared to God's display of magnificence. If God could tell the sun when it was time to set, certainly He could tell Katie when it was time to break up with Michael, with or without Christy's input. Christy silently vowed to pray for Katie and Michael every day, and she hoped she would always be able to see things in perspective— from God's point of view.

Todd slipped his arm around Christy and drew her close. "You know what, Kilikina? I've prayed a long time about us being together just like this."

Resting her head on his shoulder, Christy said, "I've prayed the same thing, Todd. You know how the other day you said that for us, right now, this is a time to enjoy?"

"I remember," Todd answered, his voice sounding low and mellow.

"I think I know a better word."

"Yeah? What's that?"

"Cherish. For us, right now, this is a time to cherish."

Christy could hear Todd's echo of agreement from her snuggled-up position against his chest. "I like that," he said, "a time for us to cherish."

Together they watched the sunset, each hearing the other's steady breathing and feeling the warmth of being so close.

"Look at the color of those clouds," Christy said softly as the last tinges of pink faded from the sky. "Did you see it? It was a sort of dusty rose, wasn't it?"

Todd must have caught her hint. "White is good for a cloud too, you know."

"But don't you think dusty rose is more of a forever, cloud kind of color?"

"You know what," Todd said, grasping Christy's hand and leading her back toward the house. "I think we have enough time to go to the paint store before dinner and buy ourselves a can of dusty rose paint. After all, what other color would you paint a 'cute,' five-dollar bookshelf?"

"Well, white is good," Christy said, teasing him right back. "But not for this one. This one is a dusty rose."

"Because this is one to cherish."

"Right," Christy agreed, gazing into the great forever beyond the sunset. "This is one to cherish."

"And so are you, Kilikina," Todd said, stopping in the sand and wrapping his arms around her. "You are the one I cherish."

Two Captivating Series from Robin Jones Gunn

FOCUS ON THE FAMILY®
LIKE THIS BOOK?